Books by Norma Johnston

THE DAYS OF THE DRAGON'S SEED

Norma Johnston

THE DAYS OF THE DRAGON'S SEED

Atheneum · 1982 · New York

Library of Congress Cataloging in Publication Data

Johnston, Norma
The days of the dragon's seed.

SUMMARY: Retells the myths of Oedipus who unknowingly
killed his father and married his mother and
of Antigone who was condemned to death for burying her brother
after he had attacked his own city.
1. Oedipus. 2. Antigone. [1. Odeipus. 2. Antigone.
3. Mythology, Greek] I. Title.
PZ8.1.J64Day   398.2'2'0938   81-10786
ISBN 0-689-30882-5   AACR2

Published simultaneously in Canada by
McClelland & Stewart, Ltd.
Composition by American-Stratford Graphic Services,
Brattleboro, Vermont
Printed and bound by
Fairfield Graphics, Fairfield, Pennsylvania
Designed by M. M. Ahern
First Edition

for Augusta W. Lamm

CONTENTS

PROLOGUE

There was in Greece, the wise ones say, a race of men and women sprung from dragon's teeth. Cadmus began it, Cadmus the son of Agenor the Phoenician and brother of Europa, who was carried off by a Zeus disguised as a bull. Cadmus, ranging the world in search of his abducted sister, traveled through Rhodes, through Thera and through Thrace, and thence to Delphi to consult Apollo's oracle.

The prophetess bid him abandon his fruitless quest. He should follow a cow, she told him, and where it lay down, there must he build a city. In Phocis, Cadmus came upon a heifer with white marks in the shape of Artemis's own moon on its flanks, and he followed the heifer across Boeotia. At last the cow lay down, and Cadmus knew he stood upon the site of his destined city. He wished to sacrifice the animal at once, so he sent his followers to a nearby spring to fetch the water for the ritual.

But this spring was sacred to Ares, god of war, and was guarded by a dragon breathing fire. All of Cadmus's companions were struck down, but he himself, guided by Athena's wisdom, stayed out of reach until he could deal the monster a fatal blow. Then, following the goddess' bidding, he plucked out the fallen monster's teeth and cast them on the ground.

Instantly, armed men sprang up from the soil. *Sparti,* or "sown men," seed of the dragon's teeth . . . they turned on the alien Cadmus and drew their mighty swords. But as they came near, Cadmus, at Athena's instruction, picked up a stone and flung it in their midst. In the dust of the plain, none could see from whence the stone came. The armed figures turned upon each other until all but five were slain.

Echion, Udaeus, Chthonius, Hyperenor, Pelorus . . . these were the Sparti who remained, and they joined themselves to Cadmus to help him build his city and became the ancestors of the five great families of Thebes.

Ares god of war was angered by the dragon's death and compelled Cadmus to serve him for eight years. At the end of this term Athena made Cadmus king of Thebes, and Zeus gave him Harmonia, daughter of Ares and Aphrodite, for a wife. All the gods were present at the wedding, the first mortal nuptial to be honored by their presence.

Cadmus reigned long and peacefully, but each generation after suffered in some way for the sacrilege involved in the dragon's death. It was rumored that a greater wrong than the dispatch of a sacred animal was involved; that Cadmus's real sin had been *hubris:* overweening pride, thinking oneself the equal of the gods. Nonetheless, the descendants of Cadmus and the Sparti, like their city, flourished and grew in power. They intermarried, and their heritages mingled into a common race.

They were intelligent and proud and strong. They

demanded only that they be masters of their own destinies and that whatever the gods dealt out to them, they know the reason why. That was their blasphemous *hubris*—or else the spark of divinity within them. It was at once their blessing and their curse.

Be that as it may, always in the numbering of their lives, there came a day or days when they made a choice that sealed their destinies and when, for good or ill, their *Why?* was answered. That, too, was their curse, and their blessing . . . or so the wise ones say.

The Day of the Oracle

I

The sky was the color of a kingfisher's back. It augured well, and so did Apollo's chariot, the sun, soaring across the azure distances. Space was infinite, here on these rocky heights, yet so clear was the air that to the young man it almost seemed that if he stretched forth his arms he could touch those golden rays. Or push back mountains. The young man, balancing easily in the jolting chariot, threw back his head. Laughter, which had been building in him as he climbed, burst forth in peal after peal that echoed down the mountainside.

The white horse, so well schooled that it needed no controls, did not even bother to turn its head. But the bondservant, clinging tightly to the teetering chariot, glanced apprehensively at his master and as quickly looked away. He thinks I'm drunk, Oedipus thought. I *am* drunk; on this air. Well, so be it! The violent anger that had impelled him on this quest had been metamorphosing all day. Now, in the early afternoon, he was filled with a euphoria greater than he had ever known. He took a deep breath, letting the tooled reins dangle negligently; and scarcely realizing that he was doing so, he began to sing.

He was Oedipus, heir and only child of Polybus, King of Corinth, newly entered into manhood and on his first

3

pilgrimage to the Delphic oracle. A pilgrimage made on impulse and in secrecy, which accounted for his traveling with just one servant. And accounted in part for the euphoria, too, Oedipus thought, grinning to himself. He knew, he had been told frequently enough, how his pride, his temper and impulsiveness propelled him into events faster than a javelin could fly.

"But I am right in this." Oedipus's jaw set. He had to *know*. It was all very well to say that royalty should rise above common rumor, that he had learned to endure taunts in childhood and must do so now.

"I did not endure those. I proved them false and empty!" More, he had twisted them around so that the term of derision had become a badge of honor. He was "Oedipus"—"Swollen-foot." His heels were scarred and swollen from some catastrophe his parents would not speak of, but with discus, javelin or sword he had made himself the best of all the youths of Corinth. And on horseback, wheel or foot as well! No fate could master him, save the fate he chose! The shadows faded, and he heard the man beside him breathe easier. But Oedipus, scanning the path running before him up the mountain, felt the resolve within him harden.

Six months ago—was that all it was? Six months ago the anniversary of his birth had been celebrated, as always in Corinth with great festival, for he was a much-longed-for only child born late in his parents' lives. But this year was special, for he was now a man; of age to rule, of age to marry, of age to officiate at sacrifices to the gods. There had been high ceremony and high hilarity. There had been games and races; there had been feasting, and there had been wine. Much wine, not only at the palace but in the tavernas with his friends.

It was in a taverna that he had heard the song.

Is he who's closest to the throne
Corinth's own, or one unknown?

The import of the words had not sunk in at first, for he had been mellow with the evening's ease. Then, as the song had grown more roisterous, his brow had tightened. "Stop! 's an insult to his majesty. I forbid th' singing. . . ." The words would have carried more power had his voice not traitorously slurred, and this fueled his anger. He took a deep breath, and the cry rang like thunder. "In the name of the king, my father, I, Oedipus, forbid that song!"

Knife-sharp silence. Then, from the far end of the room, a snicker. Oedipus whirled, hand on his dagger, and the silence vibrated.

"Sit down, man. It is nothing." His cousin's voice was a harsh whisper in his ear; he was pushed down, and an order was snapped to a frightened servant. "Refill the wine bowls, quickly."

A mist, red as the blood-red wine, rose in Oedipus's eyes. If he did not answer, did not strike out, it was because, humiliatingly, he was not able. The Furies had stolen all his strength.

He was aware of his cousin pressing him down upon the bench, of the golden wine bowl being lifted to his lips. He gulped. Someone began playing on a lyre, a different song full of mirth and innocent jollity. Two of the serving maids began to dance. The company—those that were still able to direct their hands—clapped time. Slowly, the red tide faded.

Oedipus's chest was heaving as though he'd run a race, and his muscles ached. In a still center amidst the encircling sound, he found himself staring into his cousin's level eyes.

"Sit still. Pretend you do not hear. By noticing, you attract notice and can do the king more dishonor than a drunken singer."

"That song is treason."

"Aye, if meant treasonously, which it is not. It's the wine talking, in both of you."

"If Polybus heard—" Oedipus started to rise, was stopped by an iron grip that only a much-loved and slightly older kinsman would have dared use.

"He's heard, and has wisely paid no heed. The song's been around the tavernas since you were born. That's why it's been resurrected tonight, in your honor."

"*Honor!*" As often, after the red tide receded, everything seemed specially sharp and bright. The true implication of the ditty leaped into Oedipus's outraged brain. "It's *I* they mean . . . how dare they, how *can* they suggest that I am not Polybus's lawful seed?"

"*I said be still.* No, not more wine; you've worshipped enough at Dionysus's shrine. Have some figs, they'll do you more good." The older man's eyes gentled, and his glance was even. "Oedipus, you are a man now, think like one. All those years of wedlock, stillbirth after stillbirth, and then no births at all. Finally, Polybus goes to Delphi to consult the oracle, leaving Merope here; he is gone a long time; a good many too few days after his return *you* are born, after he had been unable to father a child for years. Is it surprising that some cynics wondered whether the gods had a little human help?"

"Is that what the song meant, that my mother—?" Polybus, that wise regal mentor whose eyes always followed Oedipus with love and pride. . . . Polybus could not have treated him so, were they not son and father. Nor could Polybus the noble have treated Merope always with such high tenderness if she. . . .

He had to know.

His cousin was right. A quarrel in a taverna was no way for the king's son to seek truth or to right great wrongs.

The king's son.

He, Oedipus, who wore the name Swollen-foot as a badge of honor, had been proclaimed in both secular and sacred rites the son of Polybus and heir to the Corinthian throne.

How could he ever sit at peace on that throne if rumors said it was not his by right? How could he, as a man, know peace if those rumors rang inexorably in his own brain?

Oedipus rose abruptly, forcing a smile for his cousin's reassurance.

"Have no fear. I will cause no trouble here." He felt for coins. "See to it that the wine bowls pass again on my behalf, and say I have retired from the fray, exhausted from Dionysus's rites."

That had been six months ago. Now on the Delphic mountainside, the sun's golden rays caressed his already deep-bronzed shoulders, and a welcome breeze tantalized his short black beard. Oedipus, squinting, looked ahead toward the sacred grove. But his mind's eye went backward.

He had gone home—to the palace—to Polybus, whom, as the Fates would have it, was in the *megaron* waiting with amused concern for him to return. Polybus had given him a special private gift, a golden disk with the great seal of Corinth, heritage of Corinth's kings and premier princes. And Oedipus, not touching it, had stared across the golden surface at the older man and blurted out his question.

Polybus's response had been anger so swift and strong that it had reassured Oedipus, more than could any words. Polybus was furious about the song—not its existence, but that Oedipus had heard it; that anyone had dared sing it in his presence and on that day. His wrath had been so intense that in the morning he had ordered soldiers to seek out and punish the ill-starred singers. Oedipus, startled at his father's response and at his own, had found himself taking refuge in morning-after vagueness when questioned on the offenders' identities. He had not told. No one had told, and in a few days the subject had lapsed, insofar as public notice was concerned. But it had festered still in Oedipus's mind.

Once more, a few weeks later in deep privacy, he had tried to query Polybus, and the king's response had been austere.

"You do dishonor to me, your mother and yourself by dignifying vile rumors with your questions."

"But, Father—"

"Enough! As you honor us, you are never to call this matter to speech or mind again!"

Except that it would not go away. It had clawed at Oedipus like some ill-begotten monster, until his companions chided him for much melancholy. And then, when he had thrown himself recklessly into riding, racing, carousing at the taverna, his cousin had scolded. He had snapped back some glib retort, but his companion had known.

"It still rings in your ears, doesn't it?"

"What?"

"That song."

"Like a chant out of Hades." Oedipus had looked at his cousin, all defenses gone. "The Furies are after me. And will be, until I have answers and not questions."

In that moment, he had known what he must do.

Steeling himself, he had waited until he thought all suspicion would be gone from Polybus's mind. Then he had given out that he was going to Delphi on a pilgrimage. Corinth had sighed approvingly; such an act of reverence was quite the proper thing for a young prince entering into his heritage. And he had made sure that his closeness to his parents, his contentedness with life were matters of public mark, so that his true purpose in visiting the oracle would not be guessed.

Delphi was beautiful in the spring. The mountainside, gnarled and tortured by Earth-Shaker Zeus, was in stark contrast to the gray-green of olive groves in the plain below; and far away the river twisted like a silver ribbon. Above him, white rocks, mineral-encrusted, glistened with every rainbow color.

They had reached the walls. The white horse stopped, obedient to its training, although one impatient hoof still pawed the earth. The servant clambered down, went round the corner, returned to lead horse and chariot through a narrow gateway. Before them, zigzagging up further heights and paved with white glittering blocks of stone, stretched the Sacred Way.

A corner of Oedipus's mind whispered like the wind, *I am going to remember this. I am going to remember this all my days.* The luminosity of the air, the quality of the now-slanting light, the scent of thyme crushed beneath his sandals, the sound of birds now beginning to settle themselves in trees. From somewhere, faintly, the sound of running water. The evanescent miragelike coloring of the stones. And underneath, impalpable, insistent, a haunting smell that was neither animal, vegetable nor mineral, but composed of all and more.

They passed around the first cornering of the Sacred

Way, climbed further, passed another. They were at a great altar, white slabs on black marble. A preternatural stillness had settled on the atmosphere. For a moment, no birds sang.

For a moment, an unfamiliar sensation swelled in Oedipus. His heart pounded, his hands were clammy. He could not breathe; he was being swallowed in a cold gray mist. It was so like, and yet so different from, the red mist of his remembered rage that it was some moments before Oedipus recognized the experience as panic.

Why? Surely he was strong enough to bear the truth if the oracle said he was not Corinth's legitimate prince, but bastard-born or changeling.

"In any event, I am Polybus's designated heir. Kingship is determined by the predecessor's choice, not by the bloodline."

He did not realize he had murmured the words aloud until he saw the servant flash him a startled, apprehensive glance. He smiled, deliberately, and the man relaxed.

"This is the Great Altar of Apollo. The king has told me of it. Splendid, is it not?" He must remember to watch himself, if servants quailed without reason; moodiness was unbecoming in a prince.

The odor had grown more pronounced, and he knew now what it was—the fumes from the sacred pit over which the Pythian priestess prayed for inspiration. Oedipus stepped down.

"You need not wait here. Find yourself and the horse

some shade where the air is fresher." He nodded pleasantly at the servant's relieved expression, then stepped apart a few moments to compose himself.

Delphi. Earth's navel-stone. Holy shrine of Apollo the Light-giver and the Great Mother. It was light he had come for, was it not? For an instant Oedipus had a sharp impression that this, and not the date celebrated months ago, was his natal day. He took off his sandals—princes like commoners must show reverence on holy ground—and crossed the threshold into Apollo's temple.

There were altars, there were statues to the gods. They registered on him as white forms only, for Oedipus remembered as a priest approached him that he must make sacrifice, and he had come unprepared. He fumbled for coins in the leather purse that hung from his sword belt, and the priest, recognizing the gold's value, raised eyebrows and at once treated him with more respect. They adjourned outside to the Great Altar. A goat without blemish was produced. The priest, in tribute to either Oedipus's innate nobility or to his gold, proferred him the knife to perform the sacrifice. Remember all he had been taught; make the killing clean and quick . . . the animal trembled all over when holy water was sprinkled on it, and that was a good sign.

Follow the priest again across the threshold, past the statues. Down the steps into the *oikos* or waiting room. At its far end a silken curtain drifted restlessly. Oedipus knew what it was; the entrance to the *adyton*, the subterranean room where the oracular tripods were.

The priest rang a silver bell.

Light footsteps pattered on the stones behind them. A young girl, barely entered into womanhood, came from the temple proper, hair down her back in token of virginity. She passed them unseeingly and vanished into the *adyton*. The sulphurous smell grew stronger, was joined by the scent of burning laurel leaves and barley meal.

The priest gestured silently toward the curtain, which still stirred, ghost-driven.

Suddenly it overwhelmed Oedipus again, the wave of panic that rose, crested, crashed, carrying him with it. For a second only, he almost bolted. The second after, he was swept by the knowledge that if he ran now, he would have no peace ever. He must always know; he must always fight, rather than lie down in submission: *that,* more than "Swollen-foot," "Polybus's son," was who he was.

Firmly, he thrust aside the silken curtain and crossed the threshold.

The little room was dim. Somewhere gold glimmered. But he was conscious of three images only, burning themselves into his memory. The great rough stone, the *omphalos,* which marked the navel-spot of earth, was hung with garlands and with tufts of wool. From the deep cleft beneath the *omphalos,* the vapors rose, and perched on her tripod the girl leaned forward, looking downward, breathing them in deeply. By some trick of lighting, she looked young no more; her face through the vaporous mist was gaunt and haggard.

It was overpowering, that smell. Oedipus blinked, and

his heart was pounding. The girl's breathing was audible now and guttural, merging into moans. Her eyes rolled. She flung her head back, her gold hair wild.

The priest murmured at his elbow. "Ask what you will. The god will answer."

He had been about to say, "Am I the son of Polybus and Merope?" But he had a sudden distaste for speaking aloud their names. He said instead, "Who are my father and my mother? Are they those to whom I give those names?"

No sound, except the little priestess's heavy breathing. Her hair was like scattered gold, like a golden snare. The fumes eddied, burning Oedipus's nose and throat.

He heard himself burst out with a tortured cry. *"By the gods, who am I?"*

The girl's head swayed forward again, swayed back. She writhed in an invisible grasp. The hairs on the back of Oedipus's neck began to rise. The guttural sounds became syllables, unintelligible but filled with horror.

Oedipus swung round wildly to the priest who gripped his arm.

"I will translate," the priest said quietly. He was very still, so still that Oedipus felt his own pulse quieting. The priest closed his eyes, his head tilted back slightly, and slowly his arms rose. At first faintly, then stronger, sounds began to come from his lips also. Half-spoken, half-chanted, these were not wild mouthings but intelligible words.

"Woe unto you. . . ."

Oedipus struggled against the vapors, forcing his mind to clear. The old voice went on.

"Woe unto you,
For you are among all men a man accursed;
For you shall bring death to the king your father,
And you shall wed his lady wife your mother,
And beget children on the body of her who bore
   you. . . ."

"What do you say?"
Oedipus jumped up, sending the stool on which he had been seated crashing. The priest's eyes were still closed; his mouth kept repeating the terrible words. Oedipus grabbed his arms, shaking him, trying to bring him back to consciousness. And the vapors billowed, and the twin mists, black and red, rose and engulfed him.

The tide receded, leaving him like a shiprecked swimmer on the shore. He heaved; animal sounds came from his throat, yet he still clutched the limp figure of the unfortunate priest. The sound of the words still tolled in the sulphurous air.

" . . . you shall bring death to the king your father,
and you shall wed his lady wife your mother. . . ."

The priestess, no longer a Hecate hag but a terrified child, cowered against the rough far wall. This was not her fault, nor the priest's either . . . nor his own. In a surge of undirected revulsion, Oedipus flung the puppet figure to one side. A corner of his mind saw the man scramble up, so he was not hurt. Strange, how he could notice that and not even feel relief. Strange, how after the mists receded some things were so sharply clear. His question had been answered after all.

". . . shall wed his lady wife your mother." So he was Polybus's legitimate child, and Merope's also.

". . . *shall wed his lady wife your mother.*"

God!

Retching, Oedipus threw himself toward the curtained doorway, lurched across the *oikos,* up the steps, down the interminable length of the temple proper.

Air, at last. He stumbled with his last strength round the corner of the temple, determined not to blaspheme Apollo's altar with his vomit. In the still shade of the cedars, he flung himself to the ground.

How long he lay there, he would never know. When he came to, his servant knelt beside him, bathing his head.

The man's face was anxious, but he asked no questions. Oedipus took a mouthful of proffered water, spat, then drank deeply. He pulled himself to a sitting position, feeling physical weakness but also that curious clarity of mind.

"Woe unto you,
For you are among all men a man accursed;

For you shall bring death to the king your father,
And you shall wed his lady wife your mother,
And beget children on the body of her who bore
*   you. . . ."*

"No."

The word, like a volcano's first murmur, came from deep within him. He had come here to find out who he was; he knew now. He was Oedipus, who must have answers to his questions. Oedipus, who must be master of his own fate.

His fingers groped in his leather purse, drew out gold coins.

"Here. Take these and go home . . . to Corinth." The servant stared at him dumbly, and he forced himself to go on calmly. "Find a taverna where you can spend the night. In the morning you must start for Corinth."

"Without you, master?"

"Without me."

He must exile himself. It was the only way. For he, Oedipus, could never raise an arm against Polybus, or look with lust on Merope . . . not when Apollo's reason was strong within him. But when the red tide came . . . ? He could not know; he did not dare to know, and that was another truth he had faced today. So for the love and honor of his parents, he must flee Corinth. Must stay away forever.

"My lord, if I go home without you, it will be said I deserted and left you to be killed."

"No, my friend. Look, you must tell my father"—he could say the word now, at least, without a tremor—"tell him I have learned that for his own safety, and my lady mother's, I must go into exile. I do so as an act of service."

Everyone would believe that *that* was what the oracle had spoken. Polybus would accept it, however sadly. No one went against Apollo's oracle.

No one but he.

He had felt, hadn't he, that this was his natal day? It was more so, now. He rose in a curious calm, bid farewell to the reluctant servant, watched as he picked his way on foot down the hill past the browsing horse and on toward the outer gate. Then, alone beside Apollo's temple, Oedipus lifted his face toward the distant heavens.

"Hear me, gods! I defy the fate that you have set upon me! I, Oedipus, have said it!"

A life had ended; a new life was beginning. And the sky, which had been the color of a kingfisher's back, had turned to black.

II

Did he sleep? Probably. He did not know. Exhaustion was heavy in him, the exhaustion of soldiers on the battlefield. Mechanically he had done those things that must be done: had watered his horse and fed it, tasks normally cared for by the departed servant. Long ago Polybus had taught him that every horseman, however noble, must bear ultimate responsibility for his own mount.

In his weariness, things like his own food and lodging went unthought of, while other things were too well remembered. The stench of the sulphur fumes still burning in his nostrils. The groans of the priestess, and the priest's voice intoning terrible prophecy. The words of the prophecy, the searing dreadful words—

Suddenly, shaking with chill, Oedipus was on his feet. His trembling fingers fumbled frantically with the horse's harness as the obedient animal whinnied faintly. He could not wait for morning, any more than he could passively allow the prophecy's fulfillment. Not sleep nor wine would blot out, ever, the screaming prophetic stanza in his brain. Nothing would help but action, and the only action that presented itself to mind was to put as many hectares between himself and Corinth as was possible. Distance was a wall that could protect his beloved parents from whatever Dionysian madness might sometime engulf him.

He was putting the stars between himself and Corinth while the skies were still as cold, black and plummetless as the midnight sea.

Back down the mountainside. Back, on the twisting narrow road beyond whose edge lay what was by day a serene plain, green with olives. By night the way held dangers, but he cared not, and some ironic god protected him. There was not even any moon by which the rich gold on his chariot could be seen, and no robbers lurked watchful in the mountain caves. The horse picked its way, sure-footed, without his guiding.

Presently, the tentative fingers of Aurora's first false light poked over the distant rim of the world's edge. Soon, Apollo would harness his own chariot for its daily ride across the sky. Lights began flickering in houses that clung precariously to the rim of the road. Farmers were preparing for a day's hard labor, little caring, not even knowing that the existence of Oedipus, Prince of Corinth, had ended less than a day ago. A few hours only; in the aching interval Phoebus's sun had not made even half a circuit. In Corinth, Merope's maids would be stirring, preparing perfumed water for her bath. Polybus, an early riser, would be dressing, planning a consultation with the court elders. Somewhere, priests would be readying a sacrifice. The first sun would gild the stones of Corinth's walls and the familiar pillars of the *agora*. Corinth, which he dared never see again.

Oedipus stopped at a farmhouse and bought bread and fruit. The man sold them readily; apparently hungry pilgrims were commonplace along the Delphi road, but his price was high, and as they bartered his eyes kept darting sideways to the gilt gleaming through the chariot's dust.

Oedipus drove a hard bargain. The coins in his pouch were plentiful but would not last forever, and he must find ways to get more—or earn them. Unwashed, sweat-stained, he sat down beneath an olive tree to force a meal. For the first time that he could remember, he omitted the customary morning libation to the gods and prayer. He did not think he would ever pray again.

The meal—what he could swallow of it—choked down, he watered his steed at a nearby stream and set off again. It was still early morning, and the road he traveled grew increasingly familiar. With what confident hope he had traversed it yesterday! Now, he was no more that person; he was alone; he lacked direction, save for the compulsion that forced him from everything dear to him and with every hectare forged firmer his resolve. One thing, at least, was sure: He had no longer any shadow of a doubt that he was Polybus's and Merope's lawful son.

So far, of necessity, his route lay along the Strait of Corinth in the same direction from which he had come. Soon, soon, he would reach a dividing of the ways and must decide. North? East? Any way but southwest toward the water, across which lay home. Should he turn into the dangers of open country, or seek a city?

He could not think. He needed speed and wildness, anything that would blot out consciousness. The horse whinnied in reproach as Oedipus flung himself on its back. So must the invisible riders on Poseidon's chargers feel, streaming in waves that dashed themselves against the shore. Perhaps he would seek the sea, throw himself into it, let the breakers carry him away, whipping at him as the wind did now.

The sun was high and burning. The wind and the sweat were cold. Fire and ice, like the torments of the damned.

Oedipus dug his fingers into the horse's mane, his body plastered against the animal's neck until rider and mount were one. The animal, sensitive to every nuance, moved even faster.

Stones flew beneath those flashing hooves and crashed over the road's edge to the land far below. So narrow was the road now, and so dangerous . . . he exulted in the danger, he embraced it. The motes of dust and light danced in his eyes and dazzled.

They were approaching a place where three roads met, and he must decide. Toward Daulia? Or toward Thebes and whatever lay beyond?

He could not see clearly. Brine stung his eyes, and a cloud of dust ahead obscured his vision. A farmer or some other pilgrim seeking Delphi.

He did not want to think again of Delphi.

Oedipus's left fingers tightened in the horse's wiry mane, and with his right hand he swung his staff. Let whoever was coming look to his own safety; he would not give way.

Sunlight glinted through the dust cloud, onto gold. Onto flying plumes. A herald, ballooning with self-importance, shouted, "Pull aside!"

The arrogance, the contempt for a supposed inferior struck Oedipus like a blow.

"Pull aside yourself! I command right of way!" He dug his heels into the horse's sides.

Suddenly, they were face-to-face. The herald brandished a spear; three other guards appeared, reaching for weapons. Oedipus's horse reared in panic, and his hooves struck out. A sword flashed, too close, and Oedipus yanked frantically on the reins. "Get over!" he shouted sharply, struggling for control.

"Boy! How dare you speak so to—"

"Enough!" The dust particles separated, the light changed, and for the first time Oedipus saw the passenger in the other carriage. Tall, eagle-faced, white-haired, every rigid line of him breathed arrogance. "The young should make way for their elders and their betters regardless of whether identity is known. Drive on."

"But, Master—"

"Drive on, I say!"

The wall of herald and attendants parted; the driver lifted his goad. Oedipus's horse whirled. By automatic reflex Oedipus's legs clamped to the horse's body. His left arm swung out to grab the other horse's lead.

The driver thrust him aside with one sharp blow.

The red mist was rising, and all of Oedipus's muscles worked by instinct. The staff whistled over the horse's head to catch the driver's head a glancing blow. The driver lost control; the carriage jolted, almost spilled over, righted at last beside the road.

"*Now*," Oedipus whispered, and his mount responded.

They passed the herald, struggling vainly to soothe a terrified beast. Passed the dazed driver, blood dripping from his head. They were face-to-face, Oedipus and the older man, and into his own triumphant gaze Oedipus threw every ounce of his pride and power as a chieftain's son.

With one swift move, like a peal of martial music, the old eagle swung forward, swept up his fallen driver's two-pronged goad. Brought it down with all force on Oedipus's head.

He was blinded—by the red mist, by blood, by the Furies or by that draught of the River Lethe that often accompanies such injuries. Afterwards, Oedipus vaguely remembered swinging, swift as lightning, the staff in his own strong arm; recalled a blurred vision of the old man tumbling from the carriage. Then the mists closed in.

When he recovered, he was lying on a patch of sparse growth beside the road, looking up at a paling sky . . . the same sky that had been above him as he had walked into Apollo's temple the day before. And it was very still. Some ways apart, his own horse and the empty chariot waited quietly. The other carriage was in pieces in the road, and among the pieces five bodies lay. Nothing lived there except a frightened horse, sides heaving, lathered, splashed with blood, entangled frantically in its own reins.

He, Oedipus, was all over blood.

Slowly, he pulled himself to his feet. Slowly, murmuring reassurance, he approached the terrified animal. He brought his knife out cautiously, keeping it hidden from the horse's sight, while he slashed and slashed at the tangled leather until the snares were opened and the animal free. For an instant it stood there, as though scarce believing. Then it was off, screaming its terror, its mane and tail streaming as it vanished into the dust and far away.

Heavily, Oedipus went back to his own transport. He

climbed into the chariot, feeling as though the weight of the slain man's years had been transferred to him. For a silent moment he stood looking at the carnage. Then he picked up his reins, clucked automatically, and horse, chariot and rider rolled away.

One thing now was settled. He had passed the crossroads of the turn toward Daulia. He was headed toward Thebes. And presently the walls of that great city-kingdom rose above him.

Thebes—Cadmus's city. Here, on this very plain Oedipus was now traversing, Cadmus had slain Ares's sacred dragon. That must have been the dragon's lair, that cave from which clear water gushed through eight founts into a stone basin. All the tales learned in childhood rushed back to Oedipus's tired mind. He longed to drink deep from the bountiful spring and to wash off the dust and crusted blood. But some atavistic apprehension held him back. Not here. The dragon's imagined shape was like the image of all buried fears. There must be other springs.

He needed sleep on a proper couch, and proper food. Oh, he had prided himself so, hadn't he, on his athletic toughness? Now every muscle remembered that he was a king's son reared to royal chambers, to delicate dishes and good wine.

He would not have them long if he could not raise funds. He could not go into the city in his present state; he would be taken for a robber or worse. The horse, following its own devices, was heading up a broad road to the nearest gate, but Oedipus pulled it back onto the bypath. They circled round the base of the walled city as the sun sank lower.

Thebes of the seven gates . . . somewhere outside of them there must be water. And with luck, a taverna.

As Oedipus passed the southeast gate, the door swung open and a horse emerged, heavily burdened, led by a weathered man in traveler's clothes. A trader, Oedipus noted abstractedly, for the man's garments bore the marks of foreign cultures, and their wearer's high cheekbones and angled eyes betokened Eastern blood. And wealthy, judging by the size of the bundles, the alacrity of the doorkeeper, the small slave boy hurrying to help. Oedipus's interest quickened.

He reined his horse to a welcome stop, and the small caravan, approaching at a necessarily slow gait, saluted him. Oedipus stepped down to meet them.

The older man nodded. "A pleasant day for travel." Courteous words, spoken in foreign accent, as the other's eyes measured him without direct question.

"And a pleasant city for a night's welcome rest." Oedipus too was schooled in the sword-language of diplomacy.

"You have been hurt?"

Oedipus shook his head. "A bruised crown only. As you have seen, I encountered trouble. The roads to the North, as all know, are dangerous."

"Yet you were not afraid to undertake them." The trader gestured, and the lad ran forward with a full wineskin.

Oedipus drank gratefully. "A man who has lived with honor ought not to fear. And I had business that has brought me here." He parried the anticipated question by carrying the game into the other's field. *"You* are, it appears, embarking on a journey ill-equipped for transport."

The encounter culminated in the trader purchasing the gilded chariot. Purchasing it even though it was clear he doubted Oedipus's right of ownership.

"You drive a hard bargain," he said without rancor, watching Oedipus test the coins by biting before slipping them into the leather pouch. "Whatever your business, you will prosper at it. My way lies towards Corinth. Does yours also?"

"No."

"You head toward Chalkis, then? To trade with the bronzemakers there, no doubt. Well, good luck to you. There's a fair taverna not far down the Chalkis road. If you are wise, you'll keep your gold well-hidden, lest you not survive so well another clout upon the head."

The man left, heading south, bundles now piled comfortably in the chariot. Oedipus stood alone beside the animal that was now his sole companion.

The horse whimpered slightly and turned its head, watching the familiar chariot jolt away.

"It's all right. We don't need it," Oedipus said quietly. The velvet nose nudged his neck, and he stroked it. Then he swung himself up again on the broad back. Stabling for his steed, a couch for himself, and food for both. They began to move slowly north along the dusty path. High to their left, the walls of Thebes gleamed red-gold in the dying light. His head throbbed, and he was very tired.

The even, steady motion of the animal was lulling. He knew little else until he became conscious that they had stopped.

The city lay behind; they were on empty plain, but to the right a few trees grew. Someone had shifted stones into an altar, and beyond it from a cleft in the rocks flowed water.

Oedipus let himself down stiffly and released the horse. It went straight to drink and then drifted off, grazing quietly. Oedipus himself knelt by the spring and drank deeply, scooping up the water in both hands. Escaping drops ran like cleansing rivulets down his stained arms. Presently he immersed his aching head, then rose and stripped off his garments and scrubbed himself until at last he was clean. Then, acting on an impulse he could not explain, he fetched a grain-cake from his saddlebag and carried it and libation water to the altar stone.

The prayers he uttered were not part of the accustomed ritual he was entitled to perform, but much older ones, learned as he toddled at Merope's skirts. He felt, at once, older than his father and younger than that long-gone child.

Today he had killed a stranger. He was in flight, lest he kill someone far more close and dear. Like a child with no parental hands to guide—without even the gods whose fate he had defied—he was setting off into an unknown country. And though he knew himself now entitled to the name, he could be no more Oedipus, Prince of Corinth. It would not be safe, as a solitary traveler, to be known as a prince. But more—after all that had taken place—he would not use that name again until it was his not just by birth but by redemption in some deed of valor.

The Day of the Sphinx

III

The months passed. Oedipus had money in his pouch, and nobility as well as intelligence in his bearing, so he was accepted everywhere with respect and no overt questions. His way led first to Chalkis, that great port famed for its metalwork and for the shells much used in purple dyes. Thanks to his profit from the chariot, he was able to buy and sell; thanks to his shrewdness, his purse grew heavier rather than lighter as time went by.

The summer's heat drove him north along the Aegean. He saw Mount Olympus towering and wondered whether the gods there laughed at or were angered by his defiance. There had been no lightning bolts from on high. He heard no news of Corinth. He stayed nowhere long enough to chance such news, and the longing for his homeland grew each day.

Somewhere there must be place and duty for him fitting his birth and station, but what that might be remained veiled in mists. And for now, since he could not be where he most wished to be, it mattered little where he made his home.

He took sail to the islands, returned again to the mainland, avoiding the Corinthian peninsula as though it were a place accursed. Always he was an alien, set apart by silence and the air of mystery that clung around him; always he was made welcome, for he bore himself with dignity and dealt with others justly. His skin had turned deep bronze, and his beard had grown. When he looked at his reflection, it seemed to him a stranger's face, much older. Even his garments, bought from traders in his travels, marked him no longer as a Corinthian.

Always, no matter how pleasant the companions or how entreating the importunities of village maidens, there would come a time when visions in the night became too great to bear, and with the dawn, his saddlebags packed, he would be gone. And always he went with the hope that strange towns, strange faces, work and wine would blot out, like the Lethean stream, the memory of the curse.

It was in a taverna at the foot of Mount Parnassus that he first heard again of Thebes.

It was late at night, and the wine was flowing. The serving girls, picking their way carefully among grabbing arms, refilled the common bowls. Two other travelers, already bathed and oil-pomaded, were exuberantly dancing. Laughter and off-key singing rang through the shadows of the low-roofed rooms. Oedipus's companion, a sponge merchant from the Souinon, drank deeply and passed the wine bowl on to Oedipus as a maid knelt to slip off his dusty sandals.

"Makes a man think of settling down—at least, settling in a place that offers such pleasant solace." The man smiled, nodding toward couches where travelers had persuaded village maids to provide other consolations.

"Makes a man soft." Oedipus spoke shortly. Then, aware his tone could give offense, he shrugged and smiled. "I prefer the sterner sports that make an athlete."

Involuntarily, the sponge merchant's eyes strayed to Oedipus's misshapen feet. Oedipus's eyes blazed. The other's smile faded, and he rushed into placatory speech.

"You, it is clear, are athlete-fit. More shame to those of us who let the years and ease seduce us." His eyes roved. "You have come from a far country, sir?"

"From many countries."

"On business or adventure?"

Oedipus shrugged. "I seek neither, nor avoid either if opportunity presents itself."

"Deeds of arms?"

"If I must. I do not fear them."

"You want a man's advice, take yourself toward Corinth. Bound to be fighting men wanted there soon; the city's ripe for picking. King Polybus has no eyes for statecraft since his doted-on heir has disappeared."

Oedipus lifted the wine bowl with both hands, so that it hid his face, but he had to steel his hands so they would not shake.

"Send him to Thebes for fighting." The dancers, seeking refreshment, joined them. "*There's* adventure for the picking, if one has the wish."

"The wish for death, you mean. Are you a fool?" the second newcomer retorted bluntly. "I'd not chance that road for all the crown that's offered."

The sponge trader asked the question Oedipus did not trust his voice to frame. "What troubles Thebes?"

"*Death*. Plague and disaster, Nemesis, in the shape of a monster that stalks the city for who knows what past wrongs. All who seek entrance or exit she challenges with a riddle, and when the poor clots can't answer, she eats 'em alive."

"She?"

"Aye, the creature's female, that much is sure." There were lecherous snickers. "Tail of a dragon, haunches of a lion, wings of an eagle—"

"—an' the forepart of a woman, the part that asks unanswerable questions." More ribald laughter. Then the speaker drained the wine bowl, wiped his mouth on his arm and spoke somberly. "It's the end of Thebes if the monster's not destroyed. The city's without food, for none can go in nor out. And now with King Laius dead—"

"Where did you hear that?"

"From a traveler earlier today. He'd been set on by robbers, he and all his party. It must have been right after that the Nemesis appeared. Now Creon, Laius's wife's brother, rules. Or tries to. He's a youth and lacks ability to command obedience in such a crisis. So Thebes has sent the message out by signal fires that Laius's throne and queen shall be the reward of whoever frees the city from this terror."

Oedipus's heart was pounding. He pulled himself to his feet, carefully framing a courteous departure speech. "I have had long travel today, and I need sleep." But once out of the lamp-smoked drinking room, he turned not toward the sleeping quarters but out of doors. The moon was bright above an autumn landscape, and he breathed deeply, trying to drive out the wine fumes in his brain.

In Thebes lay death or honor. A throne for a king's son, a queen's hand in marriage, the gratitude of the populace—and surely, surely, the favor of the gods!

He could die. But better death in armed struggle in a noble cause, than this death in life, this running without identity or home, as the only alternative to a dreadful curse. And he, Oedipus, had always had skill with riddles.

He let his breath out, and exultation, like new wine, began fermenting in his veins. In the morning he would rise early. He would make, as was only proper, a ritual cleansing and a sacrifice to the gods. But he had no doubt that it was on his own wits and cleverness, his skill at arms, that the outcome of the contest would depend.

IV

The sky was white with heat as he rode toward Thebes. White was the sandy dust, and white the stones, white as bleached bones. Not a breeze stirred, and not a cloud hung in the endless heavens. The air was heavy with still waiting.

The sweat stood out on Oedipus's forehead like beads of glass. For the past endless hectares he and the horse and the landscape had been one. Yesterday he had passed the crossroads where the three roads met; and he had gone on almost without notice. His thoughts were all on Thebes.

Thebes was his destiny—he knew it more surely than if any oracle had spoken. No destiny put upon him by the gods, but of his own choosing: the encounter with the monster would be his end, or his beginning. And as he saw the wall of Thebes take shape like a mirage before him, the future beckoned like altar fires.

Higher and higher they loomed as he approached the walls of Cadmus's city. Yellow-white, gray-white, terra-cotta—they were all of these and more, according to the tricks of light; and the glittering minerals that flecked them blazed in the blazing sun. They dwarfed horse and rider, but nonetheless Oedipus felt a curious elation building in him.

At the foot of the first path, the one that led to the Bourraiai Gate, he stopped, dismounted, stripped himself as warriors did or athletes preparing for the ultimate encounter. He oiled his body, too, as they did.

From where would it come, this pestilence that he was meant to battle? Did it lurk in some hidden cave, or crouch unseen behind the rocks ahead? The word was that it let no one out nor in, so it must somehow be keeping watch on all the seven gates.

Banners hung limp on the ramparts of walled Thebes. The banners all were black.

There was a curious unreality to the landscape, and all at once Oedipus realized it was because he approached a sleeping city. No animals wandered the near countryside;

no trade caravans went back and forth; there was none of the unusual commerce of a royal city. No being, human or inhuman, was to be seen. The stench of death was everywhere. Of course—for these six months, Thebes had been unable to bury its dead, for the cemetery lay without the city walls. It was an offense against the gods and against the spirits of the deceased to leave the dead unburied, for those spirits were doomed to roam between this world and the Otherworld until the proper rites had been performed.

Oedipus had not remounted. He walked with the focused relaxation of a cat, his hand on the dagger in the swordbelt that was all he wore. His horse, perfectly attuned, followed a few paces behind without his leading.

Nothing else moved. Somewhere, the predator was waiting.

A thin thread of sound came from high above him. Rusty, like notes of music. A lone trumpet, reminding him of the pomp that had once been his in Corinth. Polybus had so doted on him in his infancy that his progress through state chambers, even on all fours, had been accompanied by royal fanfares. Now he strode on two legs, not crawled on four, and no honors marked his path, for he had no rank until he made one for himself.

What would he have in old age, when time, as it did to all, forced him to lean on the third leg of a walking staff? Royal honors, or only the benison of a seat by a nameless fire? Would he even see old age? Today would tell.

He must not allow his mind to be seduced into the inattentiveness of musings.

The faint trumpet sound grew louder. A figure, tiny in the distance, gesticulated to him from the rampart of the gate. The watcher, a guard empowered to keep eye over all that approached the city, friend or foe.

Vaguely he could discern the message. *Go back. You must come no further. There is danger here.*

Oedipus cupped his hands around his mouth and shouted back. "I seek the danger. I come to combat it."

More signals, questioning. *Your name?*

Oedipus shook his head, feigning not to understand. He would have no name unless it were King of Thebes. No one would carry back to Corinth word that Oedipus son of Polybus died in a failed quest.

King of Thebes. The musing, honey-sweet, tantalized his brain.

Suddenly, though nothing anywhere had changed, his skin prickled and the hairs on the back of his neck began to rise. A presence, invisible, but near, and coming nearer. . . .

There was a whirring like strange music in the sky, and a silhouette against the distant sun. The image, once seen, imprinted itself indelibly on his dazzled vision. Wings outstretched, it seemed at first like one of Zeus's eagles, were it not for the sinuous ribbon of tail and the curious elegance of the flying form. For a moment, Oedipus was struck dumb. Then the creature whirled; dove downward. Then it was on his back.

Its claws raked his shoulders. Its breath was at his throat, evil and cloyingly sweet, like decaying flowers. He felt no pain, though blood was running down his arms. In that instant, all that he was and could be, all that he dreamed of, came sharply into focus.

He braced himself, muscles quivering, and laid his hands on the claws that dug his flesh. They were soft, like velvet; warm, like paws, like a woman's hands. Momentarily, they were thus locked together, motionless. Then, with a surge of strength, he had torn the monster from him and flung it forward, over his shoulders, to the ground. He stood back, crouched and ready, breathing hard.

Silence. The creature did not spring. There was a curious peace about it, an acknowledgement of an adversary worthy of its match. It stretched, as a cat does in the sun, and settled into a position of watchful repose. Oedipus, equally silent, watched it. Watched *her*.

The creature was female. Oedipus had been told that. He had been told, too, that she was partly human, but now the full awareness of those facts drowned his senses.

The face was a maiden's face, but the black, slanted eyes set in the golden skin were a woman's eyes, ages old. Beneath the bare uptilted breasts her body tapered, then swelled into sleek golden fur, like some ancestral lion's. Her tail, curled neatly round her folded form, was the tail of Cadmus's dragon. Not in Corinth, not in all his travels, had his eyes beheld such terrible beauty. And more—a recognition dimly sensed that in some unknown way she was his Self, his Other—that never, should he live a thousand years, would he encounter one he could so love, so hate, so equal.

The stillness hummed, and a humming came from her as well, like a purring merging imperceptibly from sense to sound. Then a singing, catlike, varying from deep to high. Did he hear words, or did they form themselves within his brain?

Why come you?

"Seeking you."

Who are you?

"I have not yet earned my name. But I am good at fighting and at riddles."

He held his breath. His muscles tensed.

She licked her lips with a small pointed tongue, and stretched, and crouched. Not yet poised to spring, but waiting, waiting. The blood throbbed in his ears, and the exquisite singing.

What is it that goes out at dawn upon four legs, that at noonday strides on two, and that at eventide returns on three?

A giddiness seized Oedipus and an elation. The vision —it must have been a vision—that had come to him, earlier on the road, returned, and with it a surge of exultation in his own wisdom. His voice rang out.

"The creature is Man, who in infancy crawls upon the ground; who in the noon of manhood walks tall with pride; who in the twilight of his honored age leans upon his staff."

The creature's eyes flared wide. For a moment their gaze impaled each other. Then with a terrible cry, she sprang upon him.

He had thought that he was strong and fit for combat; he had thought himself equal to any trial by man or nature. *She* had an inhuman strength that equaled his, drained his, turned his legs to jelly. The cloying sweet breath was like the incense and the fumes from the Earth's navel-stone, sacred home of the Mother Goddess. He struggled with all his being against yielding, against melting into her death-embrace.

Her wings beat at him; the air screamed with the sound of them, and his blood ran from the scraping of her claws; but he felt nothing, knew nothing except the struggle and their breathing and the beating of their hearts and the burning of the sun. And the cry burst from his vitals and rang out to the ringing sky.

"I have won! You shall not destroy me for I, Oedipus, Prince of Corinth, by my own wits have solved your riddle!"

He sensed, rather than saw, the creature's struggle momentarily abate. For a moment, they were motionlessly embraced. Then, seizing on her weakness, he tore her from him, held her at arm's length, forced her down. Down on the white stones, down in the white dust, then down into a stream that flowed through an open aqueduct from the Spring of Ares. He pinioned her body with his body, her arms with his arm, locked his eyes shut and held her head with all his strength beneath the cleansing water.

Slowly, slowly, her struggles ceased. Her claws, which had been digging at him desperately, opened, trailed like a woman's fingers down his arm, and then were still.

The red mist, which had engulfed him, armoring him against her power, began to fade.

He lifted his head, turned, and looked up toward the ramparts of Thebes. The black banners had come down. A youth somewhat younger than he himself stood staring at him.

Oedipus, bloody and sweat-stained, pulled himself to his feet, and his voice rang out. "Unbar your gates and sound your city's trumpets. Thebes is saved!"

He did not look back at the still, elegant form that lay behind him.

Trumpets. The sound of many trumpets, and excited cries. Colored banners being run up on the ramparts. People, famine-weakened people, pouring out through all the seven gates to engulf him, embrace him, lift him high. Flowers were thrown at him; garlands, hastily woven, hung about his neck. He was swept on a roaring tide to the Onka Gate.

Inside the gate, the youth Oedipus had earlier seen stood atop high steps. He had dressed, hastily, in gold accoutrements and royal crimson. Oedipus whispered to the old peasant who was carrying him, "Who is that?" and the murmur, faintly contemptuous, came back.

"Creon, brother to the Queen, and Regent."

Perhaps it was the boy's youth that accounted for the condescension, for it seemed otherwise undeserved. When

Creon raised his arm, the crowd obeyed with silence. When he spoke, Oedipus's heart swelled, and he felt a kinship, a sense of at last being addressed as an equal by an equal.

"Stranger, savior of our city, Thebes bids you welcome. What brought you to us, the gods alone may know; but we shall do honor to them together as soon as you are refreshed. For now, the honors be to you that we have promised."

He swept the crimson cloak off his own shoulders and fastened it with golden clasps around Oedipus's bloodstained shoulders. An elder of the city had brought on a silken pillow a circlet of gold, magnificently wrought. It was placed on Oedipus's brow. Creon unbuckled his golden sword and held it out to Oedipus with both hands.

"The royal sword of Thebes. I have worn it, custodian of the royal power, since our King Laius died. It, and the throne, and the kingship have been pledged to whoever rid our land of the monster's power."

Across the great weapon, the eyes of the two young men met. Oedipus had the odd sensation that he was looking into a mirror of his own pride, his own royalty, his own ambition. Yet this youth, but a few years the younger, had not dared as he had; had not challenged the monster, for if he had he would be king, or dead. And that was the gulf that separated them, even as their faces kindled with liking, and their hands clasped in an unspoken pact.

A dark-haired woman, radiant in full-blown beauty, stood beside them, and Creon took her hand. "Jocasta, queen of Thebes, in whom resides, as it does in you now, the royal authority. As her brother, I give you her hand in marriage, as a sign and seal that Thebes and its people acknowledge you as king."

The shimmering gauze of her garments caressed her regal form, and her rich jewels gleamed. From somewhere came the scent of autumn roses. All his energies had been keyed for this moment, but now it came too fast. Oedipus closed his eyes briefly; opened them to find himself looking directly into her amused and knowing gaze.

Blood from his combat soaked his royal cloak, blood ran from his brow down into his eyes. Jocasta took off a delicate veil and wiped his face.

"It will be ruined," he mumbled, tongue-tied.

"It is no matter." She chuckled. "Husband—husband-to-be—do you not think it is time we learned your name?"

He cleared his throat, took a sip of proferred wine. A breeze had sprung up, cooling his aching skin. The banners around the ramparts lifted proudly.

"Madam, your servant, Oedipus, Prince of Corinth." And now King of Thebes.

Overhead, the sky was azure, full of mystery.

The Day of the Soothsayer

V

The sky over Thebes was the color of brass. It had been yellow-gray when the sun went down; and now, soon after dawn, it was equally austere. Twice seven years had Oedipus ruled in Thebes, and this year there was famine in the land.

Jocasta turned over wearily on the royal couch, sensing rather than seeing Oedipus leave her side. He had slept, though she had not; his confidence never wavered, but now a delegation of elders awaited him at the palace gate. They had been waiting there since dusk and could be put off no longer, for unrest stalked the land.

Fourteen years—there had not been a summer such as this for fourteen years, not since the sere season when Oedipus had come like a young god, bringing life and joy again to Thebes, and to her heart. Her years with Laius had been another life. Jocasta's whole existence had started over when Oedipus renewed her youth. She had been scarce out of childhood when her nuptials to Laius were celebrated; she had been thirty-five at the time of her second wedding. And if she had never told him precisely by how much she was his senior, never once, not on their marriage bed nor now, had he found her displeasing.

Their life, their joint reign—for she too held titular

49

power, though he wielded it—had been triumphant. Until this year. Until this summer, when, in grim repetition, again there was no food.

Fourteen years ago it had been a monster, Furies-sent because of some unnamed sin of Laius, that had prevented planting. This year, as in every year since then, planting had taken place. Oblations had been made to Artemis, to Apollo, to Persephone goddess of the grain. Each man of Thebes had gone out with his own woman—and she with Oedipus—and they had blessed the fields by their own bedding in them, hoping to spur Mother Earth into fertility in emulation. Only this time, through all the countryside, little grain had sprung. Little rain had fallen, and now uneasiness stirred like an unborn monster.

Creon, as much Oedipus's friend and confidant as he was her brother, had gone to Delphi to consult the oracle. He had not yet returned, and Oedipus waited, she and Creon's wife Eurydice waited, to learn what offense against the gods had brought this retribution on them. For the false heat of this day deluded no one. The year was at autumn, and the winds of winter would soon come.

But heat was heavy now, and she could not sleep. Jocasta swung her bare feet to the floor and at once a maidservant was there, eager with sandals. In the corridor beyond the silk-curtained doorway, other servants scuttled for water so that she might bathe, for the fine-spun embroidered chiton and gold earrings, for the bronze mirror and the gilded chest that contained the powders and unguents for her face. Kohl from Egypt, henna, indigo . . .

did these exquisite artifices still enhance, or did they betray the fine lines around the eyes and mouth? And why should it matter? It ill became a queen to mourn small private griefs when her city's need was so immense.

Besides, Jocasta thought fiercely, no woman was old if a small child was hers! Little Antigone, with the black hair and black eyes so like hers, was scarcely four. And golden Ismene, two years older; and Polynices and Eteocles, who had been born within the year of her remarriage—they were her pride, they filled a hungry yearning in her heart she had never spoken of, even to her husband.

Oedipus was her pride also. She was a fool to worry about the creeping of age or the creeping of famine on the city, when Oedipus the salvation-bringer was yet king.

Jocasta stood silent, permitting the maids to dress her, hearing the sounds of the gathering multitude drifting up to her window. Then, robed and elegant, she dismissed them with a gesture. But when she was alone, she went neither to the window nor the mirror. She turned to her private altar and prostrated herself before it.

Healer of Delos, hear me. Fear is upon me, fear has riven my heart, fear of what may be told. In your house of gold, hear me, the queen of Thebes, city of light!

City of light, now city of sorrows beyond telling. Sickness was rife, outstripping the inventions of medicine. There was blight in the earth, and blight in barren births. And this morning, Apollo hid his face, his chariot rays coming only, strangely, through thick veils of cloud.

Deathless Athena, daughter of Zeus, and thy sister

Artemis, and our lord Apollo, show us your threefold power in this hour as you did before. From fire and pain of pestilence wash us and make us clean.

Outside the palace, and all down the mountainside beyond the walls, the streets reeked with death. Children died, and no one wept, for by now tears were dry. And mothers like her knelt at every altar. *Hera, mother of gods, hear my prayer that my children may be spared.* She was too old now, at forty-nine, to replace a child that died. And that awareness, icy in her veins, sat like death under her proud public confidence.

In the brass-colored city, under the brass-colored sky, the elders waited. Inside the palace Oedipus paused to adjust his purple cloak before the great door swung open to reveal his royal presence. He had not looked out. He had attendants and palace functionaries to do that for him, and so he knew of the garlands on the public altar, the tufts of wool that were part of the protocol of prayer. His eyes narrowed.

Creon ought to have been back by now from that private pilgrimage known only to the two men themselves and their wives. Creon had gone by night, unattended despite his station; for in private conference Oedipus and Creon had determined that the best cure for Thebes's incipient rebellion was confrontation with accomplished fact. He had hoped to avoid a public speech until Creon had returned with the oracle's word. But one of the qualities that made him a better king than Creon would have been was the ability to assess a situation quickly from all sides. It would be politic to make a royal appearance now, and to speak from strength.

Oedipus signaled to the doorkeeper, and the bronze-mounted doors were unbarred and pivoted wide.

The court before the palace, the steps, the area around the altar were all crowded. To the forefront were the priests and city's elders. A chanting filled the air, but as his presence became known, the sound fell silent, motion ceased, so that what he saw before him was a frieze of supplication.

"Children of the dragon's teeth, of Cadmus's line—" That was the right tone, kindly authority and superior wisdom. Oedipus could feel the rabble already grow less tense. But the elders were another matter. His eyes, surveying them, were shrewd, but he kept his expression avuncular. "What is the meaning of these lamentations, of the prayers and incense? You see I have not thought fit to rely on messengers, but have come to you myself to hear your sorrows." He paused a moment to let the implication become clear—he, Oedipus, had thus graciously condescended. Then he turned to the priest whom he and Creon for some months had watched as a potential troublemaker.

"Reverend sir, by right of age it is you who should speak for all. What is the issue? Some fear, or some desire? Willingly will I hear you; I should be heartless if I shut my ears to general petition."

"My lord and king"—oh, he was wily, too, the old fox, and had a politician's gift of speech. "You see us here, young and old, from crawling babe to the old man on his stick, priests of the gods and the pick of the city's manhood." His gesture, grand and eloquent, swept toward the city. In the market place, around Athena's twin altars, beyond, out to the river were further crowds, further wool-decked boughs, further garlands. The priest straightened, and the elderly eyes looked deliberately into Oedipus's proud ones.

You know why we cry out, Oedipus. You have seen the city's affliction. There is death in the soil, death in the pastures, death in our women's wombs. The spoken voice was silky. "It was you, a newcomer to Cadmus's city, who broke our bondage to the vile enchantress. Then, with the help of the gods, you gave us back our life. We come to you now, holding you not as equal to the gods but as the first of men. Find some deliverance for us again. It would be wise for you to thus have care of your glorious name. Your diligence saved us once; let it not be said that under your rule our rise became our fall."

Oedipus's muscles stiffened. Veiled insult and veiled threat. But he did not retort. He stood, waiting, and let the priest go on.

"If you are to be king, be king of living men, not emptiness."

If he would be king. . . . Oedipus let the silence settle as inch by inch he fought back the red rage. For fourteen years he had kept it so well controlled that none save Creon and Jocasta knew of it. Fourteen of the best years Thebes had known—

"I grieve for you, my children." Automatically, from long practice, the right tone came, and also the right images. His intellect never failed him; he knew that, even if the common people chose to think he was but the instrument of the gods. "I know all you suffer. None suffers more than I, for where you have each your own griefs, the king bears the weight of all. My eyes have wept. While I have seemed idle, my mind has walked through endless ways of thought. And I have done more."

Oedipus raised his head. By a trick of the elements, at that moment a breeze broke through the clouds and lifted his royal cloak, and the gold on his sword hilt gleamed. His eyes flashed, sweeping across the crowd, catching a startled glance here, an abashed look there. A hush settled, and he knew that in that moment he seemed taller, godlike. Capitalizing on the effect, his voice rang out.

"Know you that even now our kinsman Creon, son of Menoceus, is on his way from Apollo's Pythian home. He has been sent without your asking, without your knowing, to learn what act or word of your king can bring help to our troubled city. I had expected before I spoke to you to have learned his message. Whatever the god requires, by my name and honor, it shall be done!"

He had given his oath, he had met the priest's challenge of his authority with diplomatic means, and he again controlled the situation. For the moment. Oedipus's satisfaction was tempered by the awareness that the serpent of threat was only quelled, not killed. Where was Creon? Ought he himself to have gone to Delphi, or had he been right in deeming it unwise for the king to leave Thebes at such a time? Or had the real truth been that he had dreaded the thought of facing the Pythian oracle again?

Enough of that. Long ago, in another lifetime, a young man had fled from dread predictions, retching—but everything in the years since had proved that oracle wrong. His throne, his marriage, and his honor . . . by these things he, Oedipus, had foiled the gods' intent. And would continue to do so, so long as he stayed well away from Corinth. So what needed he fear oracles—or priests? It was well, nonetheless, that he had sent his trusted Creon to the oracle. That would please the people.

Where was Creon?

Creon, jolting over stones in the narrow road, lifted his head to the skies and wondered if a storm was coming. Such a thick curtain of yellow cloud obscured the sun. He should make haste. The horses of his chariot, and of the four armed guards attendant to his station, were capable of more speed. But his heart was heavy, and he did not know why. The message of the oracle seemed so simple. And the instructions were just the sort of charge to be most pleasing to Oedipus, his king, his brother and his friend. So why did this sense of fear, emotion most unfamiliar, touch his heart?

Thebes was before him on its hillside, banners flying proudly in defiance of starvation. He could delay no longer. Creon spurred his horse and flashed forward, before his guard, up the road to the Onka Gate.

Crowds, and minor temple attendants, were waiting to lead him in. That meant word of his mission was public knowledge. What had been happening in his absence? Creon's eyes narrowed, scanned the mob even as his politic smile flashed. Yes, he had been wise to stop and crown his head with bay, full-berried. The message of that triumphal sign would even now be being carried to Oedipus, and to the priests.

His horse had been unharnessed. Men were dragging his chariot up the wide avenue, past buildings and alleys rank with the stench of death.

Oedipus was waiting before the great altar, purple-cloaked. There was going to be no chance for a first conference in private. The king's voice rang out.

"Our royal brother! What news bring you, what message from the mouth of the light-giving god?"

Trust Oedipus to give him what clue he could, the fact that the populace now knew the exact nature of his mission. Creon, meeting Oedipus' eyes, chose his words with care.

"Good news. By which I mean that good comes even from painful matters, if all goes well."

Would Oedipus understand that, though to the people the pain referred to famine, there was more on which they must speak alone? No, the great voice roared in a tone Creon knew too well. "You dangle me like Tantalus between fear and hope. Speak out, royal brother! What is the god's reply?"

It was necessary to keep the voice temperate, to give

no person ground to think him challenging or conspiratorial. "Most certainly I will tell you, if you wish me to do so publicly. If not, let us go inside."

Oedipus made an expansive gesture. With a sinking heart Creon recognized the blind, overconfident mood. This was more than politic display, it was the man's own *hubris:* overweening pride. "Speak before my people. Their plight concerns me, more than my own life."

Very well. Creon straightened, assuming the prescribed formal speech pattern like ritual armor. "This is the answer, this Phoebus's plain command. An unclean thing has been permitted to pollute our soil."

Oedipus' eyes flashed. "What, here in Thebes?"

"Aye, here where it was born and raised." I know you don't like this, but you wished to hear it, Creon thought with grim amusement. "It must be driven away lest it destroy us."

The gasps of dismay spread through the listeners to the seven gates. Oedipus seemed to grow taller, his nostrils flaring at the call to action. "What is this unclean thing? What purification is required?"

"A man's banishment of blood for blood."

From the corner of his eye Creon saw a flash of gold veil on the roof. Jocasta had come out and was listening. *Oedipus, it is time to send the mob away. Withdraw inside!* No, he could not, or would not, hear Creon's unvoiced plea. The spellbinding voice demanded, "Blood for what blood? Who was it who died?"

Blessed be the gods for the formality of public rhetoric. Creon paused, continued evenly. "We had a king, sir, before you came to rule us." *Understand, Oedipus, and pray that Jocasta cannot hear.*

He did not. He shrugged impatiently. "I know. I never saw him."

A spark of anger flared briefly in Creon's brain. Very well, let all hear. "He was killed. Clearly the god's command is that the killer must be brought to justice." Silence. Then ripples of sound. Where could Thebes uncover, now, evidence of that long-gone crime? Creon rapped out the answer. "The god said *here*. What's sought shall be found, what's unsought remains to fester."

He had Oedipus's attention now. The king's eyes narrowed, and he stroked his beard. "Where was it honored Laius met this violent death?

The crowd stirred, was silent. Even the power-hungry old priest was silent. It was to Creon that all eyes turned, and the gaze was like incense to Creon's senses. For the first time since the dark cave at Delphi, he felt relaxed. He stood erect, at ease, looking straight into the eyes of this brother-friend, this king, who sought his explanation. Jocasta, and her painful memories, vanished from their minds.

"Laius left Thebes, he said, on pilgrimage. From that day on, we set no eye upon him. He had a company of guards—all died, save one who fled in horror. That guard, returning, had but one thing to tell. Robbers, not one but many, had fallen on the party and put all but him to death."

Oedipus made a contemptuous gesture. "Robbers would scarcely dare such outrage against a king unless paid to do so."

"That was suggested. But in the troubles that followed, no one was able to seek vengeance on the murderers." They spoke now as in private, the crowd forgotten. Oedipus's lip curled faintly.

"What trouble could have been great enough to hinder inquiry into a royal death?"

Was that an implication that he, royal Creon, ought to have pursued the matter? Creon spoke very quietly. "A monster, sir, forced us to turn attention from unsolved mysteries to more immediate matters."

For a moment the two pairs of eyes, so alike, clashed, and long-buried memories sprang to life.

A faint breeze lifted the dual scents of death and incense to their nostrils. Oedipus shifted his weight slightly, causing the gold armor to glint as his royal cloak moved. He lifted his face toward the crowd below; lifted his voice.

"I, the Sphinx-slayer, will start afresh and bring buried truth to light. All praise to Apollo, the light-giver!" A gesture, crowd-calculated, toward Creon: "And to you, royal brother, our royal thanks for pointing out our duty to the dead. You will find me as willing as any as you could wish in the cause of the gods and of our beloved Thebes." Oedipus gripped Creon's arm. "My own cause, too," he murmured ruefully for Creon's ear. "By the gods, the killer of King Laius might some day think to lift his hand against

King Oedipus as well." He raised his voice again, turning benevolently toward the crowd.

"Up, my children! Take away these supplicating boughs, for your prayers are answered. Summon here all those of Cadmus's city, and let them know there is nothing I, Oedipus, will not do!"

The familiar great gesture, half-salute, half-blessing. The familiar roar of the crowd. Then Oedipus swung round and strode, alone, into the palace and the great door swung shut.

The chief priest pulled himself to his feet, his voice ironic. "Up, children. You have heard the king's promise. Now let us pray to Apollo, from whom came the answer, that he himself shall descend to deliver us."

Creon, unnoticed, lost himself in the crowd.

VI

Midday. The sky, gray gold; the unbroken blanket of cloud now weighted with the smoke of sacrifice. In the square the prayers of the populace went on under the guidance of the priests, as rumor stalked the streets.

Unavenged murder, buried nearly fifteen years. A stain upon Thebes, the death of a great king thus forgotten. In the palace, with his chief advisors, Oedipus prayed, his face somber but his heart exultant. How right, how inexpressibly fitting that at the height of his powers this call to right a great wrong should have come to him! In the private apartments the young princes Eteocles and Polynices heard the tale and dreamed of manhood, quests and glory. The royal children, golden Ismene and dark Antigone, and Haemon who was Creon's pride, sensed the general restlessness and were restless too. Creon wondered about what was to come, and in her chambers Jocasta arrayed herself in regal state for the summons to public appearance that was bound to come. She pinned her gown at the shoulders with the great gold brooches that had been part of her first-marriage dowry, and long-buried images of the past rose to haunt her mind.

From homes and alleys and more public places, from family altars and beside the dying, prayers ascended. *From old crimes unavenged, from fire and the pestilence, save us and make us clean.*

When Apollo's hidden chariot was high, the palace doors swung open to reveal a rival sun. Oedipus, gold-gleaming, raised his arm in the familiar gesture, and the familiar silence fell over a people reassured.

"Your prayers shall be answered with release and help —if you obey me. If *you* are willing to undertake the remedy the gods require."

He spoke like a god. Creon, watching, involuntarily admired the skill with which Oedipus turned disadvantage to advantage. "I your king am but a stranger to the events of this unrighted tragedy. Not as your king, but as a citizen new among you, it is to you, the offspring of the dragon's teeth, that I appeal." The shrewd, hooded, eagle eyes surveyed the multitude. "If any of you know whose hand struck down Laius, son of Labdacus, declare that now to me."

Pause. Silence.

"If any man bears a weight of guilt, let him surrender himself. In so doing, he will suffer the less. His fate will be banishment; no other harm will touch him."

Silence still.

"Perhaps an alien was the assassin. If any of you have knowledge of this fact, declare it. The informer will have his king's reward, as well as the gratitude of all of Thebes." Oedipus waited. The crowd waited for a reply that did not come. Creon saw a tiny muscle twitch dangerously in Oedipus's taut cheek. It was a sign that he had come to know, and he felt himself bracing, not so much *against* his king and friend, but *for* him.

The mist was rising, the red mist, which all the years had been banked fire, repressed not quenched. Oedipus knew this. In his blood and bone he knew, as he faced a silence that could only be defiance, that the fire had begun to blaze. With a swift gesture he flung back his cloak and strode before the altar, armor flashing. His voice rang like an emissary of the gods.

"If you will not speak, if any man is found screening his guilt or another's out of fear, I now pronounce this sentence on his head! No matter what his birth or position, low or high, he is forbidden shelter or human concourse in all this land I rule. From ritual, sacrificial rites and fellowship of prayer he is cut off. Unclean, accursed, he is expelled from every house."

A murmur of horror. Oedipus's voice, rising, overrode it. "This I will execute, for it is according to the word of the oracle none can defy! Thus shall I do my duty to the god, and to the dead. It is my solemn prayer that the unknown murderer wear the brand of shame for his shameful act, to his life's end, and that none shall be his friend. Nor do I exempt myself from this solemn curse."

He stopped, let his voice fall to an intimate private tone. "It is for you, my people, to see this sentence faithfully carried out. I am astonished that no purification was ever made for the death of one so worthy, your former king. Now I, who by your grace hold all that he once held —his throne, his crown, his bed, his wife, the children that ought to have been his—I mean to avenge him as I would the death of my own father."

A murmur again, but now of approbation. Oedipus's voice mounted on it, like a priest's. "Let no way be left untried to bring to judgment the murderer of Laius, the son of Labdacus, the son of Polydorus, the son of Cadmus! The gods curse all who disobey this charge!"

As by magic, the phrases rose fluently to his lips. "*For those accursed, let the earth remain barren, and their women's wombs. May present calamity, and worse, pursue them into Hades. But for all sons of Cadmus who are on my side, may Justice and all gods be ever with them.*"

The silence now was filled with uneasy glances. Eyes scanned eyes, searching for signs of guilt. The leader-priest stepped forth, was greeted by a titter in the crowd, which he quelled with a piercing look. His words, filled with icy dignity, were to the king. *"I am not the man, nor can I tell his name. It is the Lord Apollo who would have such knowledge."*

"No doubt," Oedipus retorted drily. "But to force a god to speak against his will is not in our powers."

"Well said, my lord. But there is one mortal who stands nearer than all others to the god of truth." The priest paused with his own notable dramatic skill. "Tiresias."

Tiresias. The name rolled like a pebble down Thebes's hill, gathering volume with velocity. Tiresias, the blind soothsayer, the old wise one . . . the only mortal, legend said, who had experienced what it was to be fully human, both man and woman. Tiresias. . . .

"I have not overlooked him," Oedipus said smoothly. He turned towards his brother-in-law with a gracious nod. "It was Prince Creon who put forth the thought. Twice this morning have I sent messengers to seek the old one, but he has not come."

The crowd was disposed to wait. It settled itself, reassured now that action had been taken. Oedipus surreptitiously shifted his weight, annoyed at the delay. Why could the infernal Delphic prophetess never give clear answer? Why was he, now, handicapped from action by the insubordination of a blind old man? His sword hand itched.

Around him his special coterie of advisors conferred, searching old memories.

"There were rumors, of course. Old wives' tales around

the fires, that Laius was killed by travelers on the Delphi road."

"I've heard that," Oedipus said shortly. "We need witnesses."

The courtier hastened to be politic. "Only a bold man will pay no heed to your curse, when once he hears it.

But would one fear words who had not shrunk from deeds? Oedipus's eyes met Creon's: *Assay the crowd.* Creon nodded in perfect understanding and slipped away.

There was a stirring in the crowd. *Tiresias. Tiresias is coming.* The rumor was borne upward, as on men's shoulders, from the Onka Gate. Oedipus adjusted his armor and went forward. The river of people parted.

An old, old man was climbing slowly, one hand on his staff, the other on the shoulder of a guiding youth. Tiresias, aged beyond all knowing, wise beyond telling. Tiresias who, blind, saw better than with mortal eyes.

As if he were reliving some moment in the forgotten past, Oedipus felt his heart begin to pound, his chest constrict. The hand that he extended automatically toward the approaching soothsayer was clammy.

"Tiresias, we, like all men, know there are no secrets hidden from your wisdom." Blessed be the gods, his voice was steady. Kingliness by now was automatic in him. "Your heart's eye sees all, sacred and profane. You know our city's plight; we turn to you as to our only help."

The old man did not respond. He only stood, implacably courteous and waiting. He knows, Oedipus thought bitterly; the old fox knows everything that's been happening here. But he won't admit it. Very well. Without a flicker of annoyance Oedipus recited the litany of the day's occurrence, like an actor playing his role.

"Spare not your skill," he finished, "in bird-lore, nor in the other prophetic arts. For your own sake, for Thebes's sake, for your king's sake, save us from pestilence. To help his fellows is man's noblest work."

Old Tiresias pulled himself upright, so that for a moment he gazed toward Oedipus with unseeing eyes. Then his shoulders sagged. "Wise words. But to be wise is to suffer. I should not have come."

The voice was a mumble, fortunately heard by few. Oedipus in an undertone responded sharply. "You show yourself no friend to Thebes if you do not answer."

"It is because I am a friend to you, because I see your words tending to no good end, that I guard my own," Tiresias answered quietly. "All here are deluded, so I will not give voice to the heavy secrets of my soul—and yours. Ask me no more."

There were twin mists, gray and red, rolling round the perimeters of Oedipus's vision like two fogs. "Insolent scoundrel!—" *Stop. Voice hoarse, unbecoming in a king. Must not speak from weakness.* "You would rouse a stone to fury." That was better; quiet with a deadly edge. "Will you stand by and see your city perish?"

Suddenly, amidst the encircling crowd, king and soothsayer were locked in intensely private communication. Tiresias' old face was immensely weary. "What will be will be,

whether I speak or not. Put your own house in order. I can
say no more."

"But *I* can. I say you had a hand in whatever evils
caused this blight on Thebes. Had you had eyes to see
with, I would proclaim that you and you alone were behind
it all!"

It was not he, Oedipus, who had shouted that accusa-
tion; it was the red mist rising. His voice had not been loud,
but it had been enough. Among the ring of figures nearest
them, silence fell. Guards reached for daggers. His words
had been ill-conceived, but he could not now withdraw
them.

Tiresias in his rags seemed to be growing taller,
stronger. The sightless eyes seemed to bore into him. "Then
hear this," the soothsayer said, so softly. "Upon your head
be the curse that you have uttered. *You* are the man you
seek."

No one had heard, the whisper was so low. They must
have heard; their non-listening was so contrived. Oedipus
held to an icy cold control and forced a contemptuous
laugh. "Your age and reputation make you think you can
make such charge, and escape the consequence?"

"Truth is my defense." Cool, fearless, the old fool
thought he could with impunity insult the king. Others
were listening—Oedipus could feel the covert glances, and
the lad whose shoulder Tiresias gripped was all big eyes.
Oedipus gave the boy a violent push and caught the old
man's arm tightly as he tottered.

"Say what you dare plainly, so all can hear your treason. *I* need not fear you!"

Air singing with tension. Eyes locked with sightless eyes. The old voice rising suddenly like a priest's in funeral wailing.

"*You* are the killer. You the man who lives in sinful union with the one you love. Who lives in pride-wrought ignorance of your own undoing. Truth alone can save you."

How dare he . . . but he would not dare, had he not been paid; had he not in some fashion been promised safety. Oedipus's infuriated brain flashed over the possibilities.

Creon. It was *Creon* who had insisted Tiresias be sent for, Tiresias who had been so long in hiding. It was *Creon* who would assume power if he, Oedipus, were overthrown, for Eteocles and Polynices were still too young. It was Creon who could have seized the throne on Laius's death, had he had bravery enough, and wisdom. Creon, his lieutenant, brother-in-law, disciple, friend.

Oedipus drew a deep breath and released his grip. "Riches and royalty, wit against wit—must envy always be the uninvited guest? It was Creon, wasn't it, who put you to this?" Tiresias shook his head, but he paid no heed. "Creon, whom I trusted—he sent you to me, the famous blind soothsayer. Tiresias *knows*, people listen to him. Your eyes are wide open to profit, aren't they? But blind to truth!"

"It was not Creon," Tiresias said patiently.

"Tiresias, the wise! What were your vaunted talents worth when the Sphinx was here? *There* was a riddle too deep for ordinary wits. Or yours! But I came to Thebes, *I*, Oedipus, the stranger. I stopped the monster's mouth. As I shall stop yours now, you old blind fool. Shameless, brainless, sightless, senseless *fool*."

Tiresias stood unmoved. "I pity you, uttering taunts that shall one day be heaped on you."

"You think you, in your darkness, can harm me who walk in light?" To his own shock, Oedipus threw back his head and laughed. "Had you eyes yet, then you would behold the king you and Creon dared think to overthrow!"

I am Oedipus. Invincible even against the prophecies of the gods.

An old man of the royal council, wise in diplomacy, was at his elbow. "Sire, it is anger that has spoken, on both sides. Surely our common thought should be on how best to fulfill the god's command."

He was right. Oedipus nodded curtly.

Tiresias, quietly: "King you are, yet in one right we are equal—the right to answer charges. Have you eyes and cannot see your own damnation? I, who serve Apollo rather than mortal ruler, tell you plainly. You have sinned, although you do not know. Rail as you will at Creon, and at me, all shame you have this day heaped on others shall descend on you."

He ought to throw the fellow, old as he was, into a dungeon. But that would disturb the people, which was not wise. Oedipus felt suddenly sickened. He made a sharp dismissive gesture. "Out of my sight, and count yourself fortunate that I let you go."

Tiresias groped for the boy, who hurried forward, and turned his sightless eyes once more towards Oedipus. "It was your wish that brought me here, not mine. Farewell. This day brings you your birth, and brings your death."

Riddles. "Must he speak riddles still?" Oedipus had not meant to speak aloud, but the old man turned.

"Riddling's your gift, your pride, your fame, your curse." He spoke so softly that Oedipus sensed, rather than heard, the words. It was a voice old as time, ringing in Oedipus's brain; it was a young girl's voice, heard long ago. It was both of these, and both were one. "The killer of Laius is here, passing as a stranger, but a Theban born. He who came seeing, blind shall he go; once rich, then a beggar, groping in exile. At once brother and father, at once son and husband. Father-killer, father-supplanter. When you can disprove this, then call the gods fools and call Tiresias blind."

When the mists receded, Oedipus was standing rigidly among his courtiers, and Tiresias was gone.

VII

In the streets of Thebes, wherever prayer was taking place, priest-led, there was a keening.

From the Delphian rock the voice of the god denounces the shedder of blood; who is the man? Let him fly with the

*speed of Poseidon's horses; Zeus's son Apollo leaps to de-
stroy. Who is the man?*

And gradually, as afternoon passed, other murmurs
entered among the prayers. *Terrible things the prophet has
spoken.* . . . *Was there a quarrel between the house of
Labdacus and the son of Polybus? We fear, but we cannot
see.* . . .

Creon, pushing cloaked and mostly unrecognized
through the narrow alleys, heard with sharp ears, frown-
ing. Impossible to believe what rumor reported Tiresias
had spoken. Impossible to believe the other rumor also
growing . . . that Oedipus had accused Creon of plotting
to seize the throne.

In the taverna to which Creon had repaired for a re-
storing wine cup, he was conscious of having been recognized. There were murmurs, swiftly hushed. He threw
back his cloak. "My fellow Thebans! I hear my brother the
king has raised a slanderous charge against me." He surveyed the group coolly, noting a hand grope surreptitiously
for a knife. "You need not fear me. If my king believes I
have done him harm by word or act, in this Thebes's hour
of calamity, I have no wish to live."

"The words were spoken in anger, unconsidered." A
big man, by his clothes a skilled tradesman, answered tem-
perately. He gave his companions warning looks. "Will you
do us the honor to drink wine with us, royal sir?"

In a short time Creon had the whole story from them
and was able from intimate experience to fill in what they

did not know. The king's temper and his pride; the king's anger bursting into words he did not mean. . . . With a heavy heart, Creon ordered another bowl of wine for the party and took his leave.

The murmurs followed him as he climbed the broad way to the palace, and the guards at the great doors looked at him askance. Creon pushed past them brusquely.

Oedipus was in the outer court, conferring with two of his ministers. Heads jerked upward at Creon's approach, and eyes were uneasy. Oedipus made an abrupt dismissive gesture, and the men left.

The two friends, king and subject, faced each other across the marble floor in which scenes of bygone conflicts formed a frieze.

"Have you the gall to come here?" Oedipus asked coldly. "To my door—I'd not have thought you'd have the courage, Creon. Unless you think me a coward, or a fool so blind I cannot recognize a plot concocted."

"There was no plot."

"Don't add insult to treachery," Oedipus snapped. "*I* have wits, if you don't. Creon, how could you think that you, with no money, with no influential friend but me, could gain a crown? Kingdoms are won by men and money-bags!"

"You once thought it was by courage, strength and brains." Creon stopped, seeing Oedipus's eyes start, then narrow. "I am sorry; I did not mean to rake up old fires. Oedipus, listen—"

"To anything, except that you can be trusted."

"By the gods, Oedipus, what wrong do you think I've done you?"

Oedipus snorted. "It was you, wasn't it, who made me bring that prating prophet here?"

"*Yes*, and I would again, because he's closest to the gods in wisdom, and you were deeply worried about your people's troubles." He did not say, *about incipient rebellion*, but the common knowledge was heavy in the air between them. Oedipus let his breath out, went to a table, and seating himself pushed a wine jug toward Creon without looking. The tension was broken for the moment. Creon sipped cautiously, watching Oedipus over the terra-cotta rim.

When Oedipus spoke again, it was in a completely different subject and different tone. "How long ago did Laius . . . disappear?"

"Longer ago than I can quite remember."

"Was no inquiry made into his death?"

"Of course. It was futile."

"And this all-wise prophet was here then, and silent?" Oedipus stroked his beard. "And in those days, he never mentioned me? Or any quarrel between the House of Thebes and the House of Corinth?"

"No."

Oedipus swung round suddenly. "Then how, without your prompting, would he have dared name me now as Laius's killer?"

Creon's hands, holding the wine jug, grew rigid. He must not provoke wrath, and that not only because Oedipus was king. But rather because he was a friend, and Creon knew wrath was the one thing Oedipus could not deal with. Creon said quietly, "You grant, I imagine, that as a citizen I have the right to question you as you have questioned me?"

A curt nod.

"You are my sister's husband? And Jocasta is your equal partner in rule and in possession here in Thebes? And I, her brother, have a third and equal share of honor?" Nods to each. Creon sat back. "Man, ask yourself! Would any rational prince exchange a life of quiet honors for an uneasy throne? To be king in name was never my ambition; to live a kingly life is quite enough. What more could a moderate man desire?"

Even as he spoke, Creon realized Oedipus would not understand. Oedipus was not moderate. He went on quickly. "Oedipus, my brother, as things are, I stand in all men's favor, am all men's friends. Why, even those seeking your favors ask my intercession, feeling it will bless their cause. I have a place of honor, your friendship, I hope your love. Why would I seek your place? What would I gain except responsibilities and irksome duties?"

And power. Oedipus did not say it, no more than Creon said that he unlike Oedipus was not Fury-driven.

Their eyes met. It was Oedipus who rose and broke the contact.

"*Someone* plots against me. And when plots are afoot it's safest to take action quickly, not wait for proof and lose advantage in the contest."

"So what do you want of me? My banishment?"

"If you're a traitor, you'd be better dead than banished."

Creon stood up. "Better to let this drop now. We are both hot with choler. When your vision clears, you'll see—"

"*I see!*" Oedipus roared. "I see you are a viper I have nourished."

"And just supposing, Oedipus, that you are mistaken?"

"I am the king in Thebes, and kings must rule."

"Not when they rule unjustly!"

Oedipus sent the wine jug crashing with a violent gesture. "Hear him, Thebes! Challenging my authority in my own city!"

"*Is it not mine also?*"

Suddenly, something that for years had been between them, unacknowledged, flared to life. A river wide as the Styx had been crossed and could never be rebridged.

In the inner court Jocasta's ear was sore from having been pressed against the painted door. Through the day's still heat she had paced in her apartments until she could no longer bear the waiting. On the roof, hidden behind silk screens from public gaze, she had heard with growing terror Tiresias' words. She had seen Creon's departure, and his return. And even in the palace fastness, she had heard the rumors.

By the gods, the rumors . . . Jocasta rubbed her

throat, feeling as though the golden collar, the very air she breathed, was choking her. Palaces bred rumors in dank corners. Queens must ostensibly never hear them; must know all, reveal nothing. She was skilled by now, was she not, in keeping secrets?

It was not the first time she had thought the weight of a crown too heavy for a mortal head.

If she were not queen but ordinary woman, perhaps she could have gone to her husband's side. But her husband was not only king, he was *Oedipus*. Who was always right, who needed nothing, no one—that was how Thebes had seen him, how he saw himself. What Jocasta knew differently, she had never let him see: not her knowledge of the rages he would not admit; not her knowledge of his need for her. Perhaps it was the difference in their ages that made him seem at times more child than husband.

That was another thing she shielded from his awareness, as she shielded the gray, the wrinkles creeping into her hair and face. As she shielded Eteocles and Polynices from the consequences of their own inherited irrationality; as she and Eurydice had jointly shielded Creon all these years from too much self-knowledge of the Sphinx.

And now this day, this terrible day, which moved like a distorted reliving of that day when Oedipus had first come. Only now, unlike then, the Fates had raised their hands against him. Jocasta knew that, with wisdom beyond knowledge; it was the reason her heart pounded, the reason the stench of death was in her nostrils despite all her perfumed oils.

Unable to bear inaction longer, she had run downstairs when she saw Creon coming. And now the voices, inaudible at first, suddenly rose, and she could wait no more. Better Oedipus resent her interfering than that he should say things he would regret but not retract.

She flung the door open on its bronze hinges and strode purposefully across the marble court.

"What on earth are you men quarrelling about?" That was the right tone, teasingly amused, and her entrance had broken the confrontation. She slipped her arm through Oedipus's. "Creon, go home. And husband, come inside. Surely this is no time for brothers to grow wroth in some small private grievance."

The men were still staring at each other, breathing heavily. Creon said softly, "Not so small, my sister. Your husband threatens me with death or banishment."

She must successfully feign surprise and disbelief.

"It is true," Oedipus said heavily. "I have caught him plotting against me, and he will not admit it."

"May the curse of the gods," Creon said slowly, "rest on me forever if I am guilty."

Jocasta's fingers dug into Oedipus's arm. "For the love of heaven, Oedipus, believe him!" She felt him stiffen; swung round frantically to hold his eyes. "For his oath's sake, believe it, and for mine! My love, be merciful, and learn to yield!"

"Why should I?"

"Because he's never played you false, and he gives his word! Is it right to cast away a friend of years without more proof?"

Oedipus's eyes turned cold. "If you believe him innocent, you believe the prophet true. And so you ask *my* death or banishment."

"The gods forbid!" Jocasta slid her hands up his arms, summoning all her guile, her charm, "I know not what you mean, but I do know my heart is racked if my brother and my husband add family strife to our city's misery."

She held him, held him, forcing the inner panic to stay out of her eyes. At last she felt the stiffening drain from him.

"Very well. For your sake, not his. Let him go, even though it mean my death or exile."

"Oedipus," Creon said gently, "your nature brings self-torture—"

"Will you get out!"

Creon looked at Oedipus, looked at Jocasta, left. Oedipus shook off Jocasta's arms, crossed the courtyard to a far fountain and flung water on his head and face.

A dizziness engulfed Jocasta. She groped her way to a bench and sat down, holding herself against a chill.

A middle-aged man appeared from one of the small rooms opening off the court. Oedipus's chief advisor—he must have withdrawn there when Creon first arrived. He must have heard.

He approached the bench, interposing himself to

screen her from the king's view; came toward her. "My lady—"

She lifted heavy eyes.

"Persuade the king to withdraw for a time, for his own sake."

There was no point in pretense. "How did it start?" Jocasta asked.

The noble shrugged. "Wild surmises. Hot tempers long held in."

"And each blaming the other?"

"Exactly so. There is no need to speak further of it, is there, madam?" Their eyes met in perfect understanding.

Oedipus was approaching. The diplomat bowed, was dismissed and took his leave.

Oedipus watched him go, then turned back, and Jocasta's heart turned over. His expression was as naked, as unguarded as she had ever seen. She went to him, putting her arms around him, and they stood motionless.

Which of them it was led the other from the courtyard, into their private chambers, she could not say.

The heavy curtain dropped in place across the doorway. Her maids were gone. She sat quietly, watching, as Oedipus went to the window and stood looking out somberly, leaning against the frame.

"Tell me," Jocasta said at last, and Oedipus turned.

"I will. You are more to me than all else in Thebes." He came toward her, stopped, walked away again. "Creon has accused me of Laius's murder."

She made her voice, like his, matter-of-fact. "Does he say it's his knowledge, or other men's report?"

"Oh, he's clever. He's hiding behind that old soothsayer he must have bribed. For why else—" Oedipus stopped.

"Why else what, my love?"

"Why else would Tiresias have dared before all of Thebes to have said I was the man? Either he was paid to lie, offered protection—in which case the only likely candidate is your brother. Or else—"

Or else Tiresias was a true prophet, and Oedipus was god-accursed.

That was it, wasn't it, what Oedipus feared? That was why he had sent Creon to Delphi, rather than go himself. *That* was the child-secret she had sensed buried in the man. He feared the oracle.

The room went light, went dark, and Jocasta was sitting spent and still as the damp mist of memory receded. "Absolve yourself." It was her own voice speaking, as something in her knew it must, tearing open old scars that hid old secrets. "Oh, my love, no man possesses the secret of divination! I know, I know. . . . *Laius* feared a prophecy, all his life he feared it, but the prediction of his death proved quite, quite wrong."

"A prophecy from Delphi?" Oedipus asked sharply. She shook her head.

"Told him by his ministers . . . that he should die at the hands of his own child, his child and mine. That was why he . . . let me have no children." Jocasta started to laugh. "Don't you see, my love? It was wrong, *wrong*—

all Thebes knows Laius was killed by robbers at a place where three roads meet."

Oedipus was looking at her with a strange blankness. She wanted to go throw her arms round him. She could not. She must go on, whatever the private cost. "The child," she said steadily. "My one child . . . it was not three days old. Laius took it and had its ankles pierced and tied together so it could not crawl and had it exposed on the mountainside to die. Because of a prophecy—a prophecy that did not come true."

A faint breeze lifted the window's silken curtain and touched her tear-wet cheek. Oedipus came and took her in his arms. His words came painfully. "I was told . . . I would bring—death to my father and . . . dishonor to my mother. That was why I fled."

They remained so for several minutes, locked in silence.

"What you have said troubles me," Oedipus said at last.

"It ought not. I spoke but to relieve you. See, my son did not kill his father; my husband was not slain by his own son. So much for prophecy."

"Not that. When you told of Laius's death, my mind went back. . . . You said, where three roads met?"

Jocasta nodded.

"Where?"

"In Phocis, where the road divides, leading to Delphi and to Daulia . . . beloved, what is wrong?"

"Oh, ye gods." Oedipus turned to her, his eyes haggard. "Laius . . . what was he like?"

"Much like you, equally tall, but with silver hair. Oedipus, what—"

"How was he traveling? In state?"

She shook her head, struggling to remember. "He was going privately to the oracle. With five men only; a servant, guards, a herald—he in the chariot, with a driver, the other men on foot. They were set on by robbers—"

"How do you know?"

"Oedipus, my arm, you're hurting me . . . one servant lived, and when his wounds healed he returned to tell us."

"Jocasta, *think*. Is the fellow still in Thebes?"

"He went back to his old calling as a shepherd. Soon after you came. He asked my permission, and I gave it. Is he important?"

"Don't you see? He spoke of *robbers*. Plural. If we can find him, and he says *robbers* struck down Laius, the people will know the prophecy was false. It was not I; one is not more than one; he said robbers, not one lone wayfarer."

"Of course, my darling." She could not understand why he still looked so troubled. But he had seized on one thread of hope, that was some blessing. Jocasta rose, holding his head against her briefly. "Rest. I will give orders that the man be found. In any event, we shall counter this new prophecy with the proven falseness of the old. A fig for divination!"

She crossed to the bell cord and pulled it, wondering why the sense of doom was so heavy in her.

VIII

Oedipus slept. The day was now far spent, but the sinking sun had not yet touched its chariot wheels to earth. Jocasta, heavy-hearted, sent out her messengers. Then she threw a veil about her head, gathered up garlands and incense, and went out to the public altar.

The square was quiet; everywhere crouched men waited, and hollow-eyed children peered from their mothers' sides. Those she passed lowered their heads in respect, but did not speak. Jocasta laid her tribute on the marble and knelt, her head on her outstretched arms.

To thee, bright Apollo, nearest to my door, is my first prayer. Come to me bringing reason, O lord of light. Dark images possess my king and husband. Present and past are no longer distinguishable to Oedipus the wise; he listens to every word that feeds his fears. And I, his wife, can do nothing to bring him comfort. *Shining Apollo, save us from the curse of this uncleanness.* The pilot of our state is sick in mind, and I am afraid.

Footsteps, coming up the road behind her to break the stillness. A male voice with a Corinthian accent speaking.

"Strangers, by your leave, I seek the home of Oedipus. Can someone guide me to it?"

Hesitation. The chief priest, making the decision the

others had deferred to him. "You stand before it. This lady is his wife and queen."

She must take her cue, like an actor called to the playing-place all unready. Jocasta rose and threw back her veil.

The stranger, gray-haired and weatherbeaten, bowed. "Blessings upon you, lady, and on all your house."

"And on you, and our thanks for your gracious greeting. You bring a petition for my husband, or a message?"

"Good news, though springing out of grief, for him and all his house. Our people of Corinth send to make him king."

Jocasta stared. "Is Polybus king no longer in the isthmus?"

"Polybus, my lady, is in his grave."

A sudden irrational euphoria swept over Jocasta like a cleansing wave. She clapped her hands quickly, sending a small slave girl running for the master. *Where are you now, O prophecies of the gods? The man my husband feared to kill is dead, not by his hand!*

When Oedipus, dream-webbed, appeared, Jocasta swung round to him triumphantly. "Hear this man's news, and tell me then what need we fear oracles? He comes from Corinth. Polybus is dead!"

"What?"

"I assure you sir." The man, garrulous, hurried with explanations. "If you must have the sad news first, then know the king has gone the way all mortals must."

"How?"

"By such illness as puts the old to sleep—that, and the years he honorably filled."

Oedipus looked at Jocasta, and she saw, within the years and dignity that were like the gilding on a marble statue, the exultant youth she had seen long ago from the city's parapet. "So, wife! You are right—what need to heed the Pythian fire, the oracular screams of prophesying birds? I was to kill my father; now he lies dead, the prophecy unfulfilled."

"Have I not said so?" If they were not in the public square, she would have seized him in fierce, gloating arms. She saw the same thoughts mirrored in his proud eyes. Then, as though a curtain had dropped across an inner altar, the fire she had seen in him went out.

"There is still another fear. My mother."

He must not speak like this before the people. Choosing the lesser indiscretion, Jocasta put one hand on his cloaked shoulder, willed him to face her. "What has a man to do with fear? Chance rules us all. The future is unknown. The wise live from day to day as best they can." He heard her, or half-heard her. She saw the shadows struggle with reason behind his eyes. Her voice dropped to a tense whisper for his ears alone. "Forget this fear of mother-marrying. Many men have dreamed so. Some things must be forgotten, if life's to be endured."

"If she were dead, you might well have said so," Oedipus retorted. "While she lives, my fear must live."

He spoke as though they were alone together in their

chambers. He was heard. The messenger was eager to be helpful. "Pray sir, who is this woman you must fear?"

"Merope, the queen." Oedipus seemed to realize at that moment how unguardedly he was speaking. Visibly he pulled himself together. To Jocasta's infinite relief, he was able to assume the polished, politic tones of royal discourse. "Apollo's oracle said I was foredoomed to make my mother my wife and slay my father. To spare them this curse, I banished myself from Corinth, and cannot return despite my people's offer of the throne."

He was speaking again, unconsciously, as a Corinthian. Jocasta pressed her hands tightly together, willing her waning strength and confidence into him. *Apollo, help us. No, not Apollo, god of reason to whom the unreasoning mists are alien things. Hecate, goddess of the dark side of the moon, come to me. Give me the gift of casting spells, that I may protect him before unknown things that must not be spoken are unalterably said.* She stood on sure stone before her own safe home and felt a whirlpool sucking at her feet.

The messenger's face, scanning Oedipus, was kindly. "Is this the fear that has kept you from us all these years? My dear young lord, I *knew* I came to do you good. And, if truth's told, to do myself good too, on your coming home—"

"*Never.* I shall never again set foot beneath my parents' roof."

"But that's the good I can bring you, sir. Oh, it's

fortunate I was the one to come, I who know you've been deceived—"

"*What do you mean?*" Oedipus checked his violence, resumed the royal façade. "Good man, for the gods' sakes, tell me."

The messenger had full audience now, and there could be no more secrets. Jocasta, a cold like the grave creeping upward from her feet, saw the old man adjust his shabby garments, making the most of the focus that was thrust upon him.

"Polybus was no kin of yours. He's not your father, any more than I. Nor Merope your mother. You were given to them—" A pause, a gratified glance at the avid listeners. "By me."

Something in Jocasta screamed for them to stop. It was too late. Oedipus stroked his beard. She knew his mind was searching for some solid fact that he could hold to in a spinning world. "Was I . . . found? Or bought?"

"Found, in a wooded hollow of Cithaeron's mountain. I was a hireling shepherd, and your rescuer." The messenger's eyes traveled down to Oedipus' feet, now hidden by royal robes. Oedipus saw it. Jocasta saw realization of significance flare in his eyes.

"Your ankles were riveted," the messenger said, proud that he could prove his story. "I set you free."

"Who had done it?" Oedipus asked hoarsely.

The old man shrugged. "I know not. Ask the shepherd who gave you to me. He was one of Laius's men."

The cold had reached Jocasta's abdomen, like the

progress of slow hemlock's poison. Oedipus did not notice. He was no longer even aware of her. His impulsive brain demanded action. He was shouting, so that his voice rolled down the city's streets. "Good citizens, do any of you know the shepherd of whom this stranger speaks?"

The chief priest had gathered about himself his robes of office. "I believe he will prove that man you have already asked to see. The queen can tell you."

Was it her own terror that made his voice seem weighted with significance? She had sent for the survivor of Laius's death-trip with such secrecy, but the chief priest knew. The city knew.

Oedipus was turning to her, speaking with instinctive cryptic formality. "My wife, *you* know the man whom we have sent for. Is that whom he means?"

"Do not ask. . . . What does it matter what man he means? It was long ago!" She was moving in a nightmare, a Hades-landscape of mists and swirling shadows and sulphurous fumes. It was all the dreams she had never dreamed, all the mist-hauntings she had never understood in Oedipus her husband. He was there, and she, and no one, nothing else was real. She grabbed at him frantically. "By all the gods, if you would not destroy us, *stop!* Have I not suffered enough?"

She could feel the bones of his arms hard beneath her fingers, but he was unreachable, hidden from her, lost in some rationality beyond irrationality. "There is nothing to fear! Even if I am slave-born, *your* honor is not impugned! I cannot leave truth unknown!"

"I beg of you—"

He threw her off, not even seeing that she fell to the ground and crouched there sobbing. His pride, his god-defying pride was raging, and that destiny in blood and bone that drove him always. "Fetch the shepherd! Leave the royal lady to recoil if she must from my low birth. However base, I must unlock its secret. I am Oedipus, the Swollen-footed! I am Oedipus, child of Fortune, giver of good, and I shall not be shamed! *I will know who I am!*"

Cries and whispers, sounds of the crowd, engulfing her like a rushing wind. Footsteps running away, again approaching. Jocasta heard this dimly, within the void of her own silence. Her chest ached, and she could not breathe. Crouched on the cold stone she hugged herself tightly, like a child in its mother's womb. The blood throbbed in her ears.

A voice, the Corinthian's voice, said, "Here is my fellow shepherd. As good a man as was ever in Laius's service."

She did not want to look. She could not help herself. Slowly, painfully, Jocasta raised her head and stared straight into aged eyes. And knew. And screamed.

Her scream ricocheted down the mountainside. It broke the paralysis that had imprisoned her, and the next moment she was stumbling to her feet, blundering around the altar. Away from the doom-bringers, away from Oedipus, into the palace, across the endless marble of courts and corridors and into her own apartments to be brought up short before a bronze panel that gave her back her reflection, hideously distorted. She screamed again.

Oedipus did not hear. He had heard her first scream, and a corner of his brain had felt a contemptuous disdain of her woman-weakness. Hinder him from learning truth at last, would she, out of shame that she might find herself wed to one base-born? As if marriage to the Sphinx-destroyer had not outweighed all else! Compulsion like a demon was driving him, but Oedipus made himself proceed with royal grace.

"Good old man—please look at me, and be not afraid to answer. Were you in Laius's service?"

The old fellow straightened with a trace of pride. "Indeed, sir. Born and bred, not bought."

"What was your trade?"

A trace of uneasiness. "Most of my life, a shepherd."

"Where did you graze your flocks?"

"Why . . . round Cithaeron, mostly."

The man tried to look away, but Oedipus held his gaze firmly locked. "Have you ever seen this Corinthian before?"

"What man, sir?"

Enough of this. Oedipus turned to the messenger. "Can you jog his memory?"

"Indeed, sir. He won't forget those days we were neighbors on the mountain, he with his two flocks and I with one." The messenger smacked a toothless mouth with appreciation. "Three seasons were we there, from spring to autumn, then I'd drive my flock back Corinth way for the winter, and he toward Thebes." He poked his mate's ribs with a jocular elbow. "To Laius's folds, was it not?"

"Aye. . . ." To Oedipus's embarrassment the shepherd made a frightened, obsequious gesture. "Old men forget. . . ."

"You've not forgotten, have you, the babe you gave me and asked me to raise up as my own?" The Corinthian, pleased at the taut stillness his words achieved, put an expansive arm around his fellow's shoulder. "Old friend, behold! Here stands your baby boy!"

"Damn you, hold your tongue—"

Oedipus thought it wise to intervene. "Come, old fellow, you need not be afraid."

"Sire, he knows not what he says—"

Oedipus' eyes narrowed. "We forgive your ill manners and poor memory, but not evasion." He made a curt gesture and two guards stepped forward to hold the shepherd firmly. "Now, will you answer our questions willingly?"

"Sire, by the gods—"

"*Answer me!* The child he speaks of—did you give it to him?"

Oedipus had his answer even before the fellow spoke. The old head sagged. "I wish I'd died that day, as I must surely now."

"No more evasions! Where did it come from? Your home, or another's?"

"Not mine."

"Then whose?"

"By all the gods, master, ask me no more!"

Oedipus's eyes impaled him. The voice came at last in a hoarse whisper.

"It was . . . a child of Laius's house."

"A slave?"

Silence, a silence that hung suspended like a curtain enclosing king and commoner. Oedipus, curiously, felt himself slipping back through time. So had he and the Sphinx gazed at each other, briefly motionless, in a circle that was somehow love. "Must I tell?" the old voice said simply, with no fear, no anger, and Oedipus heard his own voice in the same tone reply, "You must."

"It was his child, they said." There was no mistaking who was meant.

Laius.

He was Laius's child.

You shall bring death to the king your father.

"Your lady can tell you the truth of it, if she will. It was she I took you from to be destroyed. . . ."

You shall wed his lady wife your mother. . . ."

". . . on account of some wicked curse that you'd kill your father."

"In the god's name," Oedipus whispered, "why didn't you let me die?"

The old eyes looked at him with absolving pity. "I hadn't the heart, master. I thought he'd take you somewhere and raise you as his own, base-born, in some strange place where you'd be a threat to none."

Woe unto you,

For you are among all men a man accursed. . . .

He was going to be sick. He was himself, middle-aged, and also the horror-struck youth recoiling from Delphi's fumes. He choked, retching, and stumbled away from the dumbstruck mob into the palace. *His* palace. Laius, his father's palace. Small hands plucked his garments, a child's scared voice inquired, "Papa, what is wrong?" Antigone. His daughter. And his sister.

You shall beget children on the body of her who bore you.

He could not bear to look at her. He could not bear to look upon himself. He kept going, blindly, not knowing where or why, until he was before the purple curtain covering the doorway to Jocasta's private room.

Jocasta, who had given up her child to be exposed. Jocasta, who must have known. Jocasta, whose beauty must have so enchanted the then-young shepherd that he had spared the child's life for this terrible fate.

Oedipus cried aloud, and no one answered. He hurled himself at the door, but it was locked; he kept battering at it until by brute force he bent the bolts out of their sockets. The door crashed inward, and the purple curtain that hung against its inner side gave way with it and then fell again, cutting off his sight. Knowing only that he had to do it, he pushed the silk aside.

It was the garlands on the floor he saw first, for his eyes were on the ground. The garlands Jocasta had put on to approach the altar, Jocasta who had begged him not to pry into buried secrets. . . . His gaze traveled from one flower to the other, as his feet had carried him step by step up the Delphic hillside. Flowers white and red like blood, on the marble floor, and the corner of her gold-embroidered veil. It led inexorably up the gilded leg of their bridal couch to the cushions on which they had lain, begetting their misbegotten brood. She was not there. His eyes, painfully lifting, looked across the tumbled linens into the great bronze panel. It reflected his own form, harrowed, driven. And beyond, to one side, reflected something that hung swaying softly.

He heard the faint whispering, like the sound of Jocasta's silks when she came toward him in her golden sandals. He turned.

The thing that had been Jocasta swung from a rope that had been her red-gold girdle, tied to a gilded beam. The knot was clumsy. He untied it clumsily. He laid the still body—no, not on the dishonored bed, never would she rest there more—on the marble floor, and the blue marble was the color of the blue dye with which she had painted her eyes. *She,* at least, could no longer see their shame.

He straightened her delicate garments, crossed her hands on the breast where he once had nursed. In death, even with strangled face distorted, she looked younger, the wrinkles smoothed away. He could not stop looking at her, could not bear to look at her, could not bear to see the sun. Apollo's sun, which all these years had mocked him for his unreasoning pride in his own wit. He had been blind, blind.

Jocasta's chiton was fastened at the shoulders with the

heavy brooches that had been part of her child-nuptial bridal gifts. In a kind of slow motion he unfastened them, tracing their intricate carving as a child would, feeling the sharp points of the great pins. In the same matter-of-fact slow motion he lifted them and drove the two pins into his two eyes.

IX

In the court before the palace, no sound was heard. No one spoke; all were caught in some god-conjured spell. Not even the chief priest moved. It had been Antigone, alone, bewildered in a world of adults who had no time for her, who had crept unseen out of the palace to Creon's house. She clung to his hand as Creon, knowing no more than she but sensing something terrible, made his way through a silent mob that gave way to him by instinct.

He reached the altar square just as a cry rang out within the palace. It was not Oedipus. It was Oedipus's chief officer, the trusted diplomat who appeared in the doorway, like a messenger back from Hades.

"O you most honorable lords of Thebes, weep for the things you must hear, the things that you must see. . . ."

It was Creon who took charge, for not even the chief priest seemed able. Creon went through the doorway of the doomed palace, through the still courts and corridor, past women keening and men who tore their hair. Into the inner chamber where a wild man crouched by a woman's body, bloody tears running down his beard in drenching cataracts of scarlet rain. Creon saw. Creon heard the mighty voice crying out in fear and loathing for a guide in darkness, for someone who would show to all of Thebes the father's murderer, the mother's spouse.

All the palace heard, but none dared near, for Oedipus had become anathema, a man accursed. Eteocles and Polynices, the young sons, heard and half-understood and felt sick terror. It was Creon, filled in that hour with a strange majestic calm, who reached a hand into the dark, inescapable night of the king's torment. What they spoke of in that time alone, Creon would never say. But at length he led Oedipus out—as Oedipus wished and the time demanded —out through the great door to the high altar, and a cry of horror filled the square.

The riddle of Thebes's famine, of Laius's murderer, of the doom that had fallen on the house of Labdacus must be explained formally, and Creon did so. And all the time, his mind was working. The private self, compassionate, thought Oedipus's self-mutilation ill-advised. Better to die than to live in blindness. And yet—Oedipus had brought down upon himself the very fate he in his power had decreed for Laius's killer. Never again to see the sweet sight of Thebes. Never to have shelter of or converse with any of the city; never to be permitted at prayer or sacrifice. To be forever unclean. Forever exiled . . . Oedipus was crying out for banishment. Creon must answer the cry publicly, and he was not sure what was wise.

Creon chose his words with care.

"Oedipus my kinsman. . . ." How could he define that kinship—brother-in-law, nephew, and less, and more . . . "I scoff not at your fall, nor yet reproach you."

There was no need. The sight of proud Oedipus so humbled, and of Jocasta's body carried out, as became a queen, in state, spoke more than words. Through all of Thebes the air was fraught with tensions, as tangible and tangled as the strands of some intricate rope. Humility, shame, pride . . . horror, fear, pity and relief. All, in each of them—from Oedipus, to himself the next in line (for Oedipus's sons were yet too young to rule) down to the lowest slave.

Oedipus asked banishment. Creon found his answer.

"We must await instructions from the gods. We need more sure guidance."

Before the people he gave Oedipus his pledge of proper funeral rites for dead Jocasta, of care for the children: the boys who hid themselves in the palace and would not come out; Antigone and Ismene who clung to Oedipus in weeping terror. He gave his hand to Oedipus on it, in bond and promise. And then, feeling the mantle of responsibility settle on his shoulders, he led Oedipus inside, saying that piety demanded none but kinsmen should look upon such sorrow.

Behind them, the sunset sky over Thebes was the color of blood.

The Day
of Sanctuary

X

The road toward Athens ran inward from the sea, twisting
as it climbed from the rocky coast. It had been a harsh
climb in midday heat, but the fierceness of the sun was
easing now. The girl raised her arm to rub the damp hair
back, and the dust that caked her face left another streak
upon her once-white sleeve. That dust . . . it assailed their
nostrils, parched their lips, turned her father's now-silver
hair to terra-cotta. She stopped a moment, lifting her face
hungrily in search of the faintest breeze.

"Antigone?"

"I am here, Father." Antigone's voice had the patience
of long endurance. She could scarcely remember a time
when her father had not been blind. Somewhere beyond
thought, visions of a young Oedipus, dark-haired and
splendid, slumbered along with memories of a gracious
woman whom she had called mother. Almost as far away
were recollections of pillared palace halls where air came
sweetly through blowing silken curtains, where she had
played at games with her cousin Haemon. *Thebes.* It
seemed as distant, as unattainable as the banquet hall of
the gods upon Olympus. Deliberately she had banished her
childhood on the day when, still a child, she had left

Thebes to share her father's exile, and her sister Ismene had remained behind.

Time had no meaning now. She did not even know how many miles and years their wanderings had spanned. Occasionally a reflection glimpsed in a bronze panel startled her with awareness that she had grown tall and thin, the hair, black like her mother's, matted by the elements. Mostly, it was Oedipus whom she read for signs of time passing, and Oedipus had aged rapidly and inexorably. His shoulders bent permanently against wind and rain; his face, as blind men's often do, tilted upward to catch any nuance from the heavens. One hand was wedded to the perpetually probing staff; the other, like a bird claw, clutched her wrist or plucked her garments.

"Antigone?" He *could* not be so old, Antigone thought in compassionate anger, yet his voice was like an old man's voice, faintly querulous, with an underlying edge of fear. Well, he had reason.

"I stopped to catch my breath, Father." There were times her very bones almost screamed in protest that this beggar-wandering was hard on her as well, but the words died on her lips. She had sentenced herself to this exile of her own free will. She came of a house that did what inner voices said they must, regardless of the cost, and that knowledge was both her burden and her strength.

Oedipus straightened, shaking out his ragged cloak. "So tell me, child, where have you today brought your poor old father? Shall countryfolk or townspeople tonight have opportunity to please the gods by offering hospitality to strangers? Lucky are they; I ask little and am content with less."

He was being whimsical; he knew that she was troubled, although not why. She would have to be more careful in the future. Oedipus's body was aged, but his mind was not impaired. Antigone wet her lips.

"We are near some city. I see towers and a city wall, a long way off." Description came automatically; she was so used by now to being his eyes. "I think we are beside some sacred ground. It is all overgrown with laurel, olives and vines."

"And beloved of nightingales. A good omen, child. Do you hear?" He had caught the sound before her, as he did so often. An expression of peace softened the sharp lines of his face. "Is there someplace where I can sit? My bones are not as resilient as your young ones."

"There is a seat in the rock."

"Then lead me to it. You must take care of the blind old man, my child."

He could not know how often he said that, Antigone thought, teeth gritted. Surely he knew she had that lesson learned by heart. She must have more patience. What was it Oedipus had once said? That pain, time and royal blood were the three masters that had taught him patience. She had had the same three masters.

Haemon used to tease her about her lack of patience, saying it was because she was a girl.

Why was she thinking of Haemon? Or was there something in these different towers that made her recall the bygone ones of Thebes?

Oedipus's voice came to her from the shadows where she had settled him. "Go toward the town before night falls and ask someone where we are. We are strangers, and as such must learn what customs must be followed." Gentle dignity, instructing her exactly as he had on every countless afternoon before. He did not know, she did not let him know, how much more was involved—the abasement, so hard for one born royal, of knocking on doors asking for the charity of lodgings, sometimes begging in the streets for crusts of bread. Not seeing, he had been spared knowledge, and she would die before she let him know her sense of shame.

She would be spared one thing today. Someone was coming, so the first contact with the city need not be made by her.

The old man was a farm laborer, by his clothes, and charmed at the novelty of strangers. He nodded respectfully and fussed into speech.

"Sir, before you say anything, leave that seat. That place is holy ground, owned by the dread goddesses, daughters of Earth and Darkness. We call them the All-seeing Kindly Ones."

A coldness came over Antigone. She would have spoken, but Oedipus stopped her, pulling himself with difficulty to his feet. "May they be kindly to me their suppliant.

Here is the place where I must stay forever." His hand groped for Antigone's, and she took it quickly. His face, to her dismay, was illumined. "Child, you hear? It had been destined, and this is the sign."

The laborer pushed back his hat. "I'll not take it on me to drive you off, sir. 'Least not till I've had instructions from the city. All I know is, you're on sacred ground. . . ."

Sanctuary. Antigone's mind grasped the significance hungrily.

". . . possessed by Poseidon and Prometheus, Lord of Fire." The fellow, delighted to be instructive, warmed to his theme. He patted the bas-relief of a horseman. "That spot you stand on is the Rock of Athens, the Brazen Threshold. This rider is Colonus, whose name we bear. 'Tis a place not famed in song or story, but dear to us who live here."

Oedipus, courteously, cut through the wandering discourse with a query. "Ruled by the general voice, or by one man?"

"Ah, the king of the city rules here, too. His name is Theseus, son of Aegeus."

Wise Theseus, whose name was known throughout Hellas for Appolonian wisdom. Antigone's heart breathed a swift fervent prayer of gratitude and hope.

"Can one of you, someone from here send a message to him?" Oedipus asked. The man hesitated, and he added squarely, "Such little service may bring great reward."

"What kind of reward is in a blind man's power?"

Antigone's temper flared, and her father knew it; his hand tightened on hers, and he spoke quietly. "My word is not blind."

Something in his tone brought an abashed respect in their companion. He snatched his hat off, fumbling. "Good sir . . . I can see you are good, sir, though in no good plight . . . I would do good for you. Stay where you are. I'll go tell the people—not the city folk, the Colonians—and they'll decide what's best to do with you."

He plodded off at as fast a pace as he was able.

Oedipus's sightless face turned toward Antigone. "Has he gone?"

"Yes, Father. There's only I. You can speak freely."

But he would not tell her what was on his mind. He turned from her, lifting his face toward the skies.

"O thou Holy Ones of dreadful aspect. . . ."

He was praying to the Eumenides. The Furies, they were once called. Those who pursued the guilty, especially those who had shed the blood of kin or committed acts unspeakable. *Kindly Ones* . . . a revulsion, like blood in her throat, rose in Antigone, choking her, drowning her.

". . . be gracious to me, gracious to Apollo who, with the very doom he cast upon me, promised me also rest in time to come. Promised me that at the seat of the Kindly Ones I should find sanctuary and be a source of blessing."

How long had he known this prophecy and never told her?

Oedipus's voice rose in ritual keening. It still had its old power. "Earthquake, thunder, the lightning fires of heaven —these are the signs he gave. Hear, thou gracious daughters of dark night! Hear, thou Athens, queen of cities! Have pity on this poor shadow of once-great Oedipus!"

Antigone's face felt hot. "Father, enough! There are people coming."

The fire went out of him as quickly as it had appeared, leaving her feeling both relieved and shamed. "Yes . . . yes . . . I will be still. Hide me, child, hide me in the grove till we hear their talk. Better to know their thoughts before we act."

The grove was thick with greenery. She guided him across the stone portal and concealed him. Her heart was pounding. Strange that it still had the power to do so; they had played this scene so many times before. Did familiarity never dull the edge of fear?

Even the words they overheard were so familiar. "He was here. Where is he hiding?" "Some old man, a wandering foreigner." "None else would venture into the sacred space of the implacable goddesses." "How does he dare?" "*He must leave. We must not offend the goddesses. Hush, turn away the eyes, utter a prayer. . . .*"

So often this had been their reception, and so often they had crouched so, waiting for darkness when they could creep away. But Oedipus straightened, shaking off her restraining hand.

"I am the man, one of those for whom ears are his eyes."

He was standing tall, moving toward the stone portal, almost as though he could see. The people gasped; Antigone felt a paralysis grip her.

"Good city elders, you need not fear me. You behold one whom none could call well-used by fortune. See how I make my way with borrowed eyes, leaning my strength upon this one weak prop."

He reached for her, and she would not desert him. Antigone rose, head high. Like a queen . . . she was a queen's daughter, and she must behave so. Let them stare at the torn, soiled garments, the bare feet and tangled hair. The more they stared at her, the less they would at him— she moved beside him swiftly.

With her move, a spell had been broken, and the questions came—kindly-intentioned, nonetheless curious. And the warnings, warnings that they must leave the forbidden ground. *Leave sanctuary.*

It tore at her still when her father turned to her for guidance. She turned her back to the villagers, shielding him from sight, making her voice maternal. "We must obey and do whatever the customs here require." He nodded, accepting, groped for her hands. She took his and held it tightly.

When Oedipus spoke, one of her prayers was answered, for his voice betrayed no elderly uncertainty.

"Strangers, do me no wrong if I leave this sanctuary and place my trust in you."

"No one will force you, sir, to leave against your will." Presumably this was the village leader, and he was courteous. He addressed Antigone, giving dignity to her scant years. "Lady, you understand our meaning, lead him. He need not come beyond that slab of rock. There's a ledge on his left he can sit on."

She guided him, step by careful step. His sandals were worn out, causing him to stumble. She held him up. *Gods, if any of you still listen to us, do not let him fall!* She settled him on the ledge and turned toward the elders, refusing to cringe outwardly, knowing what was coming. The sympathetic warning to the stranger: *Beware; while on our land, hate what we hate, love what we love.* The questioning: *Where are you from? Why your plight? What your name?*

The answer. The gasp of horror. There was no place in all of Hellas where the name of Oedipus was not known, where the curse on those who dared befriend him was not feared. Antigone saw, as she so often had before, the recoiling, the conferring, hands grasping for stones. This time, something unfamiliar flared in her, like a red mist, newborn, uncoiling.

Before she knew she was doing it, she had stepped forward.

"*Sirs! Just and reverent men!* Have pity! If not on my poor father, whose deeds were none of his devising, then on me! Only for my father's sake I plead. Hear me, as you would a child of your own flesh." Her voice broke, and she hated herself for it. "You are as gods to us. We have no other help, no other hope. Have mercy on us, for your gods' sake. The gods led us here . . . no one living walks any way save that the gods have set."

She could not go on. The leader looked at her compassionately. "Daughter of Oedipus, we pity you no less than him. But we fear the gods' retribution, as is only wise."

"Is this the vaunted godliness of Athens?" Oedipus's voice rang out with sudden fire. A rage was in him, a rage that both terrified her and filled her with rejoicing at its crashing life. He groped for her fiercely, pulled himself up with the aid of her rigid arm. "Athens, city of justice, city above all others where the suffering stranger can turn for help and refuge? What are you afraid of? My very name? My strength?" He brandished a withered arm. The crowd fell silent. Antigone turned away her eyes.

"My strength has been in suffering, not in action! I did not know which way I went! It was the gods, the gods who wove the trap! Do you fear my name? *I* do not. I know now who I am. I am Oedipus of the swollen feet, cast-out son of Laius and Jocasta! And many's the time I have wished that I had died there on Cithaeron's mountainside, the times I have cursed the benefactor who saved my life. I am Oedipus, among all men a man accursed, for I brought about the death of the king my father and wed my mother and begat children on her! But I did not know!"

The great voice rang out, the dimly remembered voice the child Antigone had loved in Thebes.

"My wife was a *gift*—my city's gift, a prize for slaying the Sphinx! The father whom I killed, unknowing, sought to kill me first! The law acquits me, ignorant of what I did!"

The mountains shook with the roar of the royal voice. It reached the skies. For a moment he stood so, invincible, powerful as he once had been. Then a tremor shook him, and he was again the frail old man. Antigone caught him and eased him down upon the ledge; and when he spoke again, it was in the old man's voice.

"I have your pledge that if I left the sanctuary you would not darken the bright star of Athens with an impious act. My presence brings you blessing and not danger. When the king your master comes, you shall understand. Till then, do me no harm."

Antigone could not speak. Over Oedipus's hoary head her brimming eyes did so, and the leader nodded.

"We will say no more. The king must be your judge."

"Will he come?" Antigone whispered.

The man smiled. "News travels. There will be rumors on the way. When Theseus hears the name of Oedipus, he'll come." He signaled to the others, and they withdrew apart to wait.

There was nothing to do but wait. Antigone knelt by the stream that ran through the sacred grove, splashed water on her face. She dipped the end of her shawl into the stream and went over to wipe her father's dusty brow. Effort must be made so that the king of Athens would be met with what shreds of dignity were possible. The cloth, itself travel-stained, left streaks on the weathered skin, and Antigone sighed. She did not even attempt to make herself look appealing; it was no use.

The group of Colonians, tactfully settled on the far side of the road, stirred and murmured faintly. A faint cloud of dust appeared in the distance and Antigone straightened, shading her eyes to peer. The king? No, a woman mounted on a colt. A woman with face half concealed by a broad Thessalian hat. Yet the lines of the slight body were burningly familiar, and the triangular smile on the pointed face—Antigone's heart tightened as in a vise. Then she was running, laughing and sobbing, down the road.

"*Ismene!*" It *was* Ismene, a young woman now, and beautiful, in delicate dress and golden curls that glinted in the waning sun as her hat fell back. Ismene jerked on the reins and slid down as Antigone reached her, and they clung together.

"Sister! And my father . . . oh, my dears, I have found you at last. And now I can scarcely see you through my tears." Ismene was laughing as she wiped her eyes, a silvery laugh that stopped abruptly as her eyes fell on Oedipus, arms out and groping.

"Ismene . . . daughter . . . ?"

"It is I, father." Ismene slipped down to her knees beside him. The glance that met Antigone's dark gaze was filled with shock, but her voice did not betray it.

"Why have you come, my child?" Oedipus was not guiled. He never was. Antigone could have told Ismene that. Ismene reached one hand to father, one to sister.

"So. At last, we three joined in sorrow . . . I had things to tell you that must come from my mouth alone. And so I came, with the only faithful servant that I have." Her eyes went to the colt, now placidly munching grass.

How had she known where to find them, Antigone wondered. But of course, they had been fools to think all Hellas would not be aware of their tortuous journeys.

Oedipus frowned. "Your brothers? Why are they not with you in an hour of need?"

"They are . . . where they are." Again, Ismene's eyes met Antigone's. A message transmitted: all was not well.

Again, Oedipus knew. "What do they do, ape the Egyptian fashion, where the men sit home with embroidery while their women labor? They have let you two bear all the burden of my calamity. Antigone, since on the brink of womanhood, an old man's nurse, roaming the wilds with me through sun and storm. And you, Ismene, in these wandering years risking your life to find me whenever any oracle concerned me." His rant subsided, his hand worked on hers. "What message now, Ismene? You have brought me word?"

"Oh, Father." Ismene stopped and swallowed. Antigone's dry eyes burned at her. *Tell us.* She went on. "You know how Creon ruled in Thebes, after—after. . . . When you were gone, at first it was the same. But then—Eteocles and Polynices grew to manhood. They desired the throne—"

That was why Creon had banished Oedipus, wasn't it? After all those years, when passion was spent and a measure of peace had come. Because he had sensed a power-threat from his nephews and had thought with Oedipus banished there would be less danger of the people's rallying behind his sons.

"I should not think," Oedipus said ironically, "that

Thebes would welcome kings of their black birth upon the throne."

Ismene did not answer that. She said carefully, "After they got power, it was agreed—peacefully—that they should share the throne, each to rule in turn. Only when Polynice's first term was over, he would not surrender the throne . . . Eteocles seized it. Polynices went to Argos, it's said to raise an army."

The implications battered against Antigone's brain.

"And did you think," Oedipus inquired with bitterness, "the loving gods would save me?"

"The oracles give hope of it. Father, *hear* me." Ismene shot a look over her shoulder at the waiting Colonians and went on in a swift whisper. "The people of Thebes want you back, for their own safety. The prophecy promises that where your body rests, people shall grow to greatness. Our uncle Creon will come for you soon, you'll see."

"What will be his purpose?"

"To set you close to Theban soil, though you may not touch it. Thus they can possess you, for if harm comes to your grave, it comes to them."

"They might have known as much without prophetic teaching," Oedipus said grimly. A color was coming to his face, more sign of vigor than Antigone had seen in many days. "So, they seek to lay me away in Theban burial, do they?"

Ismene shook her head reluctantly. "Blood-guilt forbids that. But they want you near. They seek your welfare, father. That means something."

"It means they care more for their skins than for mine, which saved them in an hour of great need. Thebes shall not have me." Oedipus struck his staff upon the ground, turned toward Ismene sharply. "My sons—my sons know of the prophecy?"

Ismene's silence was answer, and confirmation—Eteocles and Polynices each cared more about having the throne themselves than about their father. Oedipus's fingers dug into his daughter's arms. He pulled himself upward, like an old eagle.

"May no god mitigate the bitterness of their fated battle! The bloody warfare that they both intend, had I the power I would have it so that neither should return to the Theban throne. I was their father. They lifted up no hand to rescue nor defend me though they heard charge and sentence and my doom. *I was their father*—no more! No more."

Astonishingly, he did not waver at the expense of passion. He threw off their hands, groped his way by the light of his own anger toward the road. The group of Colonians stirred; the leader, seeing him approaching, rose.

"My friends—you have been friends thus far to me in my need—if you will stand beside me to implore boon of those stern goddesses who dwell among you, your land shall profit, and punishment shall strike my enemies down."

"What would you of us?"

"Advise me how to make amends to the divinities whose land I trespassed."

The instructions came—libations from the spring, in

delicate vessels to be found beside the shrine. The leader of the Colonians would bring them lamb's wool newly shorn to cover brims and handles according to the rite. Three libations, of water and honey only, and only the last one to be emptied wholly. Thrice nine sprays of olive, laid on the shrine with both hands while the prayers were said.

Ismene rose. "I will do what is required." A man stepped forward to lead her to the place. The leader went for wool, returned. An attendant thus far unseen stepped forward to lead Ismene into the center of the sacred grove.

They waited. The sun sank lower.

"The king is coming." "The king." It was a murmur at first, and then grew louder. Far down the road toward Athens the slanting rays glittered off a chariot's golden wheels. A proud horse swirled up, stopped obediently, stamping.

Theseus. Theseus in gilded armor, his face filled with a different radiance, grave and calm. Something in Antigone, for the first time in many years, grew still, for here there was no fear. Theseus stepped from the chariot and came toward Oedipus with sober courtesy, and his guards waited respectfully, the Colonians waited.

"The son of Laius. From all I have heard, long and often, you are no stranger to me. The wounded face, the pitiful dress confirm, sad Oedipus, that you are he. Speak freely. There is no circumstance so dread I would not hear it. I, like you, was reared in exile, and I do not forget the danger and loneliness and need for friends." Theseus held out his hand, to take Oedipus's in it firmly. "You are a man as I am, and at the end of life death shall claim us both. I will do for you what I can."

It was a meeting of equals. Two men—no, two kings, Antigone corrected herself, eyes stinging. She had never known her father as a king.

"Theseus, your noble kindness permits brief answer. My story you know." Oedipus paused. He could feel the late sun warm upon his face, and something else—from the sun, from the king before him, or from within himself. A kind of peace. "I come to offer you the gift of my tortured body. Sorry sight, but of value more than beauty."

"What value?" Theseus asked quietly.

"A blessing from my dying." The peace was growing, spreading, like the green tendrils of a vine thrusting up from ash. He had found it at last, his destiny—not to run from prophecy, or to wrestle it into change, but to be its bearer. To be the means, through all things known and unknown, of another's blessing. Oedipus's shoulders went back as he took a breath. Somewhere in his brain he could hear a voice, a strange, familiar voice that was self, mother, daughter, Sphinx and prophetess, all of these and none. "You shall know my meaning when I am dead and buried, not before."

"That is all you ask?"

"That, and to rest in this place forever."

"It is little."

"Not so little, sir."

Theseus's voice quickened. "You mean your sons? If

they seek to take you back to Thebes, would that not be better than foreign exile?"

"They do not want me. They fear my absence. They fear their retribution on this very land."

Oh, he had Theseus's attention now. "What trouble could come between my land and theirs?"

"Time. Time, my friend, the invincible, inexorable, which wreaks havoc everywhere. Only the gods live forever. All else changes." He heard his voice ring out as in the old days. Sensed the respect. More—*trust*. It was as it had once been, and yet so different. Pride gone, there were new companions: peace and wisdom. He lifted his face toward the forgiving skies and let his voice go soaring.

"Kin to kin, friend to friend, city to city, nothing is constant, all things change. Between you and my city all is fair, but Time has many and many a journey yet to run. Then my cold body in secret sleep shall drink hot blood. If this be not so, Zeus is not Zeus, Apollo not Apollo. But no more now. Enough that you should know my presence brings a blessing, not a curse."

The Colonian elders were murmuring in affirmation. "This has been his promise from the first."

Theseus's eyes swept from them to Oedipus, standing calm, to the girls, waiting. A smile softened the grave face. He turned back to the villagers.

"The kind intentions of such a man as this must be respected, not for the boon he brings only, but for hospitality and the goddesses' sake. Such claims compel me to offer sanctuary. While he stays here, I appoint you his protector. Or if he choose, he shall come with me to Athens."

Athens. Athena's city. A palace, baths, soft couches, food and wine.

Oedipus shook his head. "God reward you, but this is the place where I must vanquish those who cast me out."

"Is that the boon your presence brings?" Theseus asked wryly.

Oedipus was somber. "It follows, if you keep your word."

"You have my word. No oath could bind me more."

Theseus bowed and turned away, and Oedipus knew it. His voice cried out in panic. "You will leave me?"

"I must. You have no cause for fear. No one will take you away without my leave. You have my name to shield you, and even more, you are in Apollo's hands."

Theseus stepped into the golden chariot, turned it round and was gone toward Athens in the dying light.

The Day of
Cursing

XI

Colonus was a lovely land. Nightingales nested in the leafy vales and thronged in the deep arbors of wine-dark ivy. Their song was like the sound of Orpheus's lyre to Antigone's weary brain.

She slept on the ground, upon soft fragrant grasses, for she would not leave her father's side. And Oedipus, listening to the old curse he had placed on those who harbored Laius's killer, listening to prophetic inner voices, would not leave the sacred grove for the comforts of Theseus's palace. Ismene stayed with them, and their needs were met by kind villagers who each day brought wine and food. There was the spring to bathe in, there was the peace of sacred spaces all around them.

Presently, with the passing of the days, came Creon.

They saw, from afar off in the whirl of dust, the glint of armor. Creon had come armed and escorted by the Royal Guard. As the phalanx of men approached in tight precision, the group of villagers who constituted themselves as Oedipus's protectors rose. They stood blocking the road in silence.

Creon had not anticipated this. Antigone knew this as Creon signaled his chariot to halt and surveyed the motley group with appraising eyes. Creon had changed in the years since she left Thebes. Or perhaps it was her own too-rapid maturing that made her see him now with sharper eyes; perhaps the change had come gradually during all the years since Oedipus's fall. He was kingly now, the mantle of authority sat firmly on him. When he spoke, it was not to his kin but to his challengers.

"Gentlemen of Colonus." He had learned diplomacy, and his tone was genial. "Your looks betray alarm at seeing me. You need not fear. I am too old for violence, too aware that the city of Athens is a power second to none. No, I come in peace to bring the poor fugitive here back to his native land. Be pleased to fetch him."

The villagers shifted uneasily, unsure of what to do. For a moment Antigone, unnoticed, stood rooted, cold. Then she whirled to tell Oedipus, warn Oedipus. There was no need. Oedipus, with hearing sharpened by his eyesight's absence, parted the greenery that had concealed him and stepped out. He stood motionless, implacable, the sunlight sparkling on his silver beard.

Creon sensed his presence and turned. It was Creon, for all his air and attributes of power, who diminished somehow, as the two who had once been so close faced each other.

"Oedipus, poor unhappy man." Creon stretched out his arms.

But that's wrong, a voice in Antigone's brain said oddly. Father is not unhappy now. Creon is. Why?

"To see you cast adrift like this, a vagabond . . . and Antigone, poor child. Never would I have believed she'd come to this, a beggar, condemned as endless nursemaid to a sad old man, unprotected. Wasting her maidenhood when ripe for marriage into some proud house."

Creon had not talked that way before. Creon had not been pleased when his own son had looked at her with eyes of longing. Haemon had liked her. That was one of the things she had not let herself remember.

"Come home," Creon was saying. "Your people ask for you, and with good cause. Most of all do I." *Your people.* Creon had not said that either, not through the years of public shame. Nor had he said, banishing Oedipus after seven years of suffering, what he did now. "We are all to blame. All of our family are accursed, not you alone. Here in the light of Athens' day it must be said. Oh, Oedipus . . . by the gods of our fathers, hear me, and come home."

For Antigone, it was as if she was seeing at once two Oedipuses, two Creons. The private men, in whom heart spoke to heart as brothers. The political men, who spoke politically.

"You devil," Oedipus said, quietly.

The air shimmered, as at a call to arms.

Oedipus went on, still in that conversational tone. "There was a time when what my hand had wrought so sickened me I *begged* for banishment. You would not grant it. But then, *then*—when passion was spent and reason worked its healing, when my sons grew to manhood and my daughters flowered—*then* you drove me from my home and city. Little you cared for familial closeness then. And as for mutual guilt—" His voice roared out. "Is there no argument, Creon, you will not twist to your purposes? Do you think you can trap me again into that snare? Where were you, kinsman, in my years of hunger? You come now and find us here, welcomed, respected, thriving. And you want me back? If someone denied you everything you asked, then when all your heart's desire had been elsewhere granted, turned around and offered charity, would you take it? I lost my eyes, Creon, but I found my wits. You want me not in Thebes, but on your border. You need me there as a talisman against attack!"

Something in the air changed. Creon's eyes narrowed. *Oh, Father,* Antigone thought in panic. *Now he is certain you know the prophecy. And who could have brought it but Ismene?* Where was Ismene? She had gone into the vale to gather food. If only she would not come back until Creon's men were gone. *Artemis, protect her. She has not yet grown hard like me.*

"I am sorry for you," Creon said at last. "Your years have not yet taught you common sense."

"Go your way. I'll go mine. Hard as it may be," Oedipus said ironically, "I prefer it."

"You always did like the sound of your own voice. Much talk, much nonsense—"

"You consider yourself a model of sensible brevity?"

"Do you really think your grandiose renunciation does me more harm than you? You always were a fool when passion seized your wits!"

"*I'll* speak in passion!" Oedipus's shout shook the

trembling trees. "You think I cannot read, better than you, the state of Thebes? All my life I have had the surest guidance. Zeus, Apollo—I know now to heed them! You come with such guile to use me! You'll not have me! My everlasting curse upon your country! As for my dutiful sons, their heritage in Thebes shall be no larger than the earth they die on!"

The crash of swords crackled in the war plain of the skies. Oedipus lifted his sightless face. "The gods confirm it! The sound that was promised to me as a sign. Be gone, Creon! Be gone to your soft palace and uneasy sleep. I have done with you."

Deliberately, he turned his back. The row of silent Colonians shifted position slightly, toward Creon's guards. Creon's face, as he looked toward Oedipus, betrayed emotion only for a moment, then became a mask.

"There are other ways," he said softly. He snapped his fingers. A banner flashed a signal. Up from the vale came two guards, holding a golden-haired figure between them firmly. *Ismene*—

Antigone threw herself toward them, and brutal arms grabbed her, dragging her toward the chariot. She screamed. The few Colonians launched themselves at her captors but were held back by swords.

"The *man* is yours, the women mine," Creon snapped. "I have the right. It is war between our cities if you raise arms against me."

War, just as Oedipus had foretold.

"Take them to Thebes," Creon's voice called curtly.

Hands lifted Antigone none too gently into the chariot, and the vehicle catapulted off. She tried to throw herself from it, was caught, bit down viciously on the arm that slammed her back. A man's voice cursed. A man's fist knocked her backward against the chariot frame. She went down into darkness.

When she came to, a firm back was supporting her. A courteous Athenian voice addressed her as Princess, inquired if she was all right. She was on horseback, riding toward Colonus on the pommel before an Athenian guardsman. Ismene, half fainting, was riding with another guard beside her. Behind them, Creon's men lay in the road nursing wounds.

Theseus had come. Theseus, performing sacrifice to Poseidon at an altar beside the sea, had heard their shouts of terror. Theseus had arrested Creon, for Creon had insulted him, had defied the laws of Athens and of the gods. Creon had violated the right of sanctuary, seizing them and attempting to seize Oedipus likewise. There was bad blood now between the House of Athens and the House of Thebes.

It was Theseus himself, reining up beside her on his dappled steed, who told her of the curse Oedipus had put on Creon.

Thou fiend, who have torn the last poor lights, my children, from my darkness, may the Sun which is the eye of the gods reward you! May you and your issue alike be impotent, dwelling in darkness until you die!

Some foreboding in that made her shudder, but it was

not real now, nothing was real but the motion of the horses, the sound of distant thunder, and at last Oedipus reaching out hungry arms to hold her tight. She was safe. Ismene was safe. Athens and Theseus had protected them. But from this day on, there was death-danger between Thebes and Athens; between them and her uncle Creon, whom Theseus in mercy released and sent on his way. It was not Theseus who would bring the doom of the gods down on proud Creon.

Antigone ran her fingers through her hair, trying to shake off the dark images that assailed her. Oedipus, releasing her and Ismene after a last tight clasp, turned to their savior.

"My friend, my daughters owe their lives to you. The gods reward you and your blessed country, for nowhere else have I found justice, godliness and truth. None but I will ever know how much I owe you."

Theseus, moved, reached out to clasp the old man's hand. At the touch, Oedipus drew back sharply, and a look of infinite desolation crossed his face. "Do not touch me. I am a man corrupt with foulness. Only those of my own blood can bear that burden. Take my thanks upon you, not my stain."

The expression in Theseus's eyes made Antigone's throat tighten. When he spoke at last, his voice was matter-of-fact and calm.

"A piece of news has come to my ears on which you can advise me. At Poseidon's altar, the very place from which your need had drawn me, a suppliant sits. How he came there, no one seems to know. Not from Thebes. But he claims to be your kin. Is there anyone who would come seeking you from Argos?"

Ismene gasped. Oedipus made a distraught gesture. "My dear friend, tell me nothing more."

Theseus' face became alert. "Is there danger? Tell me."

"It is my son, sir. My worst enemy. The man whose voice I would most hate to hear."

Theseus the just looked at him oddly. "He makes supplication. We will let him do no harm. Surely a father's duty, and respect to the god to whom he makes supplication, compels you to listen. Nothing more."

Polynices, whom Ismene had said had gone to Argos. Polynices, the tall, stalwart brother who had ridden her on his shoulders an age ago when she was small. Antigone heard her own voice, impulsive: "Please, Father! The king is right, it is our duty to the gods. Give not wrong for wrong. Let him come."

Oedipus turned sightless eyes toward her, and the defiance went out of him. "The very sound of his voice is intolerable . . . but you are right. Let him come. But by your word, Theseus, guard our lives."

He came weeping. Polynices, weeping. Polynices, tall and athlete-hard, bronzed by the sun, a man now, no more the youth that she remembered. Black-bearded, armed and weeping.

Theseus had gone, but he had left guards waiting in the shrubbery should they be needed. They were not needed. Polynices came alone. He stopped several lengths away and squinted toward them, shielding his eyes against the late slanting light. The air was sultry, and somewhere in the distance lightning crackled.

"My sisters! Oh, my sisters—" Polynices held out his arms, and somehow they were running into them. He held the girls to him tightly. "What can I say? Who is more to be pitied, my father or I, for this unhappy plight that kept us so long apart?"

Now they were walking, arms entwined, brother between two sisters on the white Athenian road toward the white-haired old man who stood waiting. For a strange moment Antigone was able to see her father with a stranger's eyes—Polynices' eyes . . . the threadbare poverty of his garments, the white locks tousled by the breeze, the blind, lined face that might have been carved from stone. Was Polynices shocked? He would have been more so, something in her whispered viciously, if he had seen them when first they came to Athens. She was not sure what she felt.

Polynices' voice was penitent. "Wretch that I was—I treated you heartlessly. I was young, I knew no better then. . . . For what is past, there can be no remedy. But as we are men, Father, and as we both seek mercy of the gods, can you who are elder be merciful to me?"

Oedipus did not speak.

"No answer? Not even a word? You will not even tell me what provokes this anger?" Polynices glanced at his sisters, then back at the implacable figure that stood before him. "I claim the protection of Poseidon at whose altar this country's king granted me leave to speak. Father, hear me! I am here in exile because I claimed my birthright as your son!"

Ismene's eyes met Antigone's.

Polynices didn't notice; he was hurrying on with rising confidence. "I had the right to sit upon your throne. But Eteocles expelled me! Somehow he got the city on his side. . . . I went to Argos; I've married the daughter of King Adrastus of the Dorians; and I've made sworn allies of the best fighters in the Peloponnese."

Still Oedipus did not speak, and after a moment the younger man went on. "Now do you understand, Father? I ask your blessing on my righteous cause. For the sake of your daughters, for your own life's sake, give up whatever anger you hold against me and aid me in gaining vengeance on my usurper. You understand vengeance. . . . You and I are homeless outcasts, condemned to begging shelter, while the usurper laughs at us both. I will have vengeance, and the oracles say victory will lie with the one whom you bless. With your aid, Father, I will have success, restore you to your rightful place, and take my own."

"My rightful place." Oedipus's voice was scarce more than a whisper; quiet, musing. His sightless face, turning towards Polynices in the gathering twilight, was serene too with the serenity of one to whom darkness and danger are now old friends. "What is my rightful place, in your view, Polynices? And your own? You held the scepter and the royal throne in joint covenant with your brother. It was you who refused him the term you had compacted. It was you, coveting that throne from Creon who sat upon it, who made him drive me out. You made your father a homeless vagabond. The pauperhood at which you profess to weep—it was your gift. You who come begging to me now, taught me to beg! Had I not had daughters whose never-ending care nursed me to life, I would have been long since dead. *They* are my sons!"

The sky darkened. Clouds scudded across it like Poseidon's horses racing in the foam. Oedipus lifted both arms, like some old priest at a primitive rite.

"I cursed you once before. Curses are the lessons by which the impious learn. May you never defeat the land that bred you. May you never lie at peace in Argos. May you, dying, kill your banisher and, killing, die by him who shares your blood. I have no sons! In the name of the Father of Darkness, in the name of the goddesses on whose ground we stand, this is the blessing that you have from me! Now go, and tell your allies, tell all on the streets of Thebes what gift King Oedipus gives you!"

His arms fell. He turned and went into the grove as the rain began to fall.

Polynices stood, staring after him, as the rain ran down his body like drops of blood.

"All this for nothing. And all of our high hopes."

Antigone made a faint, involuntary cry, and he turned toward her. "Oh, my sisters, if ever these curses fulfill themselves in act . . . if ever you come again to Thebes, remember me. And do me such service as the gods would wish."

Ismene was silently weeping.

"Polynices—" Antigone caught at his arm. "If you have raised an army, send it home. Give up your struggle for the throne."

"Impossible. If I play coward, how will troops ever follow me again?" A faint smile softened his austere face. "Do not worry about an old man's curse."

"How many of your men will follow you when they've heard what is foretold?"

"Probably none. So they will not hear. With or without his blessing, I will sit on the throne of Thebes. Or die trying—which would be more honorable than to lie in fear. My father would understand that, though he'd not admit it. No, sister, save your tears. Remember only what I've asked of you, if need arises. May the gods be good to you, sisters. God knows you deserve it."

He flung his cloak about him and started off toward Athens without a backward look.

The Day of
Storm

XII

The seasons changed. Snow blanketed the vale with gentle whiteness, and in the springtime crocus and narcissi bloomed. Years passed, not many, but each one an age. Antigone grew taller, and Ismene more beautiful. The people of Colonus continued to bring their gifts, and it was known through all the land of Athens that the wise refugee at the Eumenides' shrine brought the city blessing.

Oedipus aged.

Antigone saw this, month by month, telling herself her fears were but sick fancies of her mind. His bones stiffened; his voice grew hoarse; he strained to hear. The second springtide that had flowered in him now was gone.

It was as the summer waned that she most saw these changes. The heat was heavy, holding a death-grip on a wasting world. Their garments clung to them. The flowers of the earth shriveled under the scorching sun, and it seemed at times as though Oedipus's wits shriveled with them. He lay upon his pallet, almost too weak to move, murmuring of things his eyes alone could see.

Antigone, bathing his head with water Ismene had fetched from the spring, felt something akin to terror, and a deep pity. What things Oedipus spoke of, if they were real at all, were beyond her ken.

There was no news of Thebes, no news of Polynices.

It was on a day when the air was heavy with the scent of autumn roses that Oedipus sat up suddenly.

"She is waiting."

"Who, Father?"

"Do you not see her? Crouched and still . . . sunlight on the iridescent feathers. . . . She knew that I would come."

He sank back, an inscrutable smile upon his face. Over his head, Antigone's eyes met Ismene's.

"I'll take a turn," Ismene said quietly. "You walk."

She needed exercise. All her muscles screamed. Antigone bathed herself, but there was no relief; she prayed, but there was no solace. The hours passed slowly.

In late afternoon, Colonian friends brought figs and grapes, but Oedipus did not eat. He sipped water, gazing off to scan the skies for signs they could not see. The sun sank. Birds twittered, and a faint breeze sprang up.

"Send for Theseus."

Her father's voice was such a whisper that Antigone was not sure at first that she had heard it. She turned toward the pallet. Oedipus, more alert than he had been all day, was propped up on one elbow, his eyes feverish. "Send a servant for Theseus, do you hear me?"

Servants—his mind was wandering again. She fought back the lump in her throat so she could speak calmly. "Father, be still. Rest, and no doubt the king will come tomorrow."

"Send! It is going to storm!"

"There is no sign of—"

Thunder crashed.

A wave of unreasoning alarm swept through Antigone, and she saw the same thing mirrored in Ismene's eyes. Ismene caught up a cloak and a broad hat.

"I'll go." She took a lamp and vanished.

Thunder crashed again, nearer, and lightning crackled. Oedipus's clawlike fingers dug into her arm. "Dear child, brave Theseus should be here."

She started to ask why and stopped. *The prophecy.* The gods were sending their summons to Oedipus across the sky, and he wanted Theseus there.

The rain began. The heavens clamored, and sky-fire sent terror creeping across her scalp. Where was Ismene? Would she reach Theseus, and would he come?

Somewhere beyond the sacred space, out toward the road, the ever-present company of Colonians were praying. Partly in fear of the elements, partly as though they knew. *Merciful gods, have mercy on us all.* . . .

Theseus was there. Theseus, his garments soaked, raindrops glittering like jewels upon the gold. Oedipus sat bolt upright.

"Thanks be to the gods, you have come as I desired."

His voice, uncannily, was the voice of a young man, and his mind was clear. Antigone's eyes stung. Thanks be to the gods, whatever else befell them, his mind was clear.

"What is it, son of Laius?" Theseus asked quietly.

"My hour is near. The gods have sent their couriers . . . peals of thunder, meteors, all heaven's armory." Oedipus gripped Theseus's hand. "I would not die unfaithful to the pact I made with you."

Theseus looked at him and nodded slowly. "I will do what you ask. I have cause to know the truth of your predictions."

The old hands held the strong ones tightly, the old body struggled to stand. Ismene cried out. Antigone put forth an arm to stop him, then let it fall.

"Is it night yet?"

'No, Father."

"Dark day, how long it's been since you were light to me! Farewell!" They emerged from shelter, and Oedipus lifted his face to the storm as to a joyous stream. He felt with bare feet over the ground beneath him, settled his weight confidently, let go of Theseus's arms. "Come, my daughters. It is my turn now to be your guide, as you have been for me."

He moved unerringly, following some inner vision. Ismene groped blindly for Antigone, and they followed. And Theseus. . . . Through the clearing, past the stream, the altar, deep into the sacred grove. To the brink of the chasm, where the gods' brazen staircase plunged to the roots of earth. At length he sat down, calling for water from the stream.

Antigone and Ismene brought it, sensing his purpose and that it was the last service they could do him. And Oedipus, as he had done long ago when approaching Thebes and the Sphinx's challenge, put off his garments, bathed himself, poured water- offering.

Thunder pealed, the voice of the god of gods. Ismene cried out, and a shudder ran through Antigone. Her traitorous knees gave way and she sank down, sobbing, although her eyes were dry.

Her father's arms went around her. Her father's voice, the voice of the young father the child in Thebes had loved, said, "Do not be sad. This is the end of our burdens and of all our sorrows."

She clung to him tightly. The world whirled; darkness closed in, then light; and it seemed as if from somewhere a voice was calling.

Theseus was lifting her to her feet.

Oedipus was making Theseus swear to look after them when he was gone. Oedipus was embracing her and Ismene, telling them as he had in childhood that they must be brave and good.

Oedipus was speaking like a king, the son of kings.

"Son of Aegeus, what I now unfold is a thing your city must keep to its secret heart till the end of time. I shall take you alone to the place where I must die. None else must know it. Tell no man where it lies, and it shall be a source of strength to your people forevermore. What follows, you alone shall see and know. And when your life is ending, you shall tell it to one alone, your chosen heir. And he to his, and thus on forever. So shall our covenant ensure forever your city's defense against the Children of the Dragon's Seed."

The heavens spoke. Oedipus lifted his face, and in that moment in the flare of lightning, he was young, the young hero who had set out to seek a destiny. Antigone's eyes closed against the sight. When she opened them much later, Oedipus was gone.

Theseus stood alone, holding his hands before his face as though he had seen what eyes could not bear to look on. Then he saluted heaven with one short prayer and, turning, went to Antigone and Ismene to take them in his arms.

It was over. Nothing remained but to weep and to bear forever the curse that was in their blood. Antigone shook her head in disbelief.

"While he was here, we could help him bear it. Now . . . now what we have seen and felt is past understanding."

The faithful small band of Colonians was waiting as they emerged from the sacred grove. The leader stepped forward, he who had been Oedipus's friend.

"What happened?"

Antigone only looked at him. "He died."

"How?"

"Not in war. Not by sea. Something—carried him off to that dark shore. And just as dark as death shall our night be." Antigone stopped, shook her head as a child might, puzzled. "How odd . . . even the loss of sadness is a loss. There was a joy in sorrow, when he was here. . . .

Well, he had had his wish. He had come to a land he loved, and in its cool curtained bed of earth he lay. There were tears for him, but not in her eyes. Her tears had all been shed. Her father was gone, and she did not know where he had been laid.

"You know his end was happy," the old Colonian voice said, being comforting. "Your grief must not be endless."

There was no comfort. No comfort, and no sure end. Antigone's head jerked up. "We must go back—"

Ismene stared at her, startled. "Antigone, why?"

"To see where he is. I cannot leave him."

"We can't go back. It's forbidden."

"Why do you cross me?"

"Don't you see?" Ismene captured her hands with gentle firmness. "He had to die alone and have no tomb."

"Then take me to the place that I may die there also!"

"And what shall I do, alone without you? Where shall I be safe?"

Two pairs of dark eyes stared at each other across a deepening void.

It was Theseus who broke the tension, putting a hand on each to lead them toward the road. "Daughters—" How like him, the kind friend, to feel that now he must fulfill a father's role. "Death has dealt gently with him. We must not weep."

Ismene nodded, choking back tears. Antigone only looked at him with burning Theban eyes.

"Let me see our father's grave."

"I cannot."

"You are lord of Athens. You can make it possible."

A look—of what? Amusement? Pity?—crossed Theseus' face and then was gone. He answered her soberly, as an equal. "It was your father's charge that no mortal should approach the place, nor living voice be heard about the sacred sepulcher where he sleeps. That pact, preserved, protects the land of Athens and brings it blessing. I gave your father an oath before the gods."

Antigone nodded. "It's his wish. It's enough. Then do this more for us. Send us safe to Thebes."

Perhaps there they yet could stem the tide of blood that doomed their brothers.

Ismene lifted a startled face, understood, and was silent. Theseus considered, nodded.

"It shall be done. I cannot rest until I have served your father and you in every way I can."

Overhead the storm had stopped. The heavens were still. Somewhere, a nightingale sang, and Artemis's chariot, the moon, drove that virgin goddess across the skies.

This was the end of tears, of lamentation. Whatever lay ahead of them down the corridor of years, this night's event was immutable and fixed. Oedipus, son of Laius and Jocasta, was at last at peace.

The Day of
Burial

XIII

In Thebes, Eteocles ruled in uneasy peace. Creon, counting his options, took Ismene and Antigone into his own home and kept his counsel. At length, Haemon asked Antigone's hand in marriage, and Creon thought it expedient to give consent to their bethrothal. Time had passed; the horrors of Oedipus had been forgotten, and all that was remembered now was his wise rule.

Polynices was still in Argos. News came to Thebes from time to time of alliances and plotting. Creon waited. The old ancestral curse was working itself out, and there was no telling yet which way it would turn.

At length, the time was ripe.

The armies of Polynices gathered—seven allies, each with his army. Amphiaraus, mighty with spear and master of augury, brother of Polynices' bride Aegia. Capaneus and Hippomedon, both of Argos; and Eteoclus; and Mecisteus brother of Adrastus, Aegia's father. Tydeus, of Calanon in Aetolia; and Parthenopaeus, the Arcadian son of Atlanta. Through bribery, through treachery, through ambition, and through old loyalties, these nobles joined with Polynices to lay siege on Thebes. Across Hellas they marched, to drums and trumpets, to the walled city of the dragon's teeth.

Gods, and too-loving women, helped them. The news

traveled to Thebes by traders and by signal fires. Thebes prayed, and Eteocles gathered up an army.

Hosts ranked in thousands ringed the thresholds of the seven gates in a circle of blood. At their head, Polynices swooped like a ravenous bird of prey with white wings flashing and with flying plumes.

Heat in the white heavens built over the white plain. Above the seven gates the proud banners hung limp, and motes of dust shimmered in the still air. Inside the walled city, Eteocles and the defenders girded themselves for battle, and Eurydice prayed. Haemon and Antigone clung together in the walled garden and planned their wedding, seeking to blot out dark visions of what might come.

The trumpets called, and the immortality of heroes beckoned; out through the seven gates rode Eteocles, claimant to the throne of Thebes, and all his army, to lift arms against his enemy, his brother. The flashing armor of the seven armies was a stream of gold, surging up from the pale gray-green of the olive groves. The clash of sword on sword, of shield on shield, the scream of horses, mounted to the heavens. Ismene took refuge at Eurydice's private altar, trembling. Creon watched from the parapet, wondering what he would have done did he deem himself still young enough for battle. Haemon was out among Thebes's defenders, wielding a bloody sword, hoping the fates would not call upon him to be the slayer of his cousin Polynices, his beloved's brother. Antigone paced, alone.

As streams of blood ran down from the heights of Thebes to form one river, Zeus, god of lightning, came to the aid of the children of the dragon's seed. Down from the heavens, home of hurricanes, swung Zeus's onslaught. Thunder roared and dust rose like a thick curtain in the blinding light, though no rain fell.

At length merciful night cloaked all in blackness. The attackers withdrew warily to their small fires, the defenders into the city, in an uneasy tension to await the dawn.

With the morn, the brightest of suns dawned upon the city of the seven gates, and a great quiet lay over the blood-soaked plain. Then the city's defenders knew that they had been saved. The remnant army, triumphant, went out to despoil the bodies of the enemy dead, stripping gold and bronze to lay on the city's altar in gratitude to Zeus.

Eteocles, defender of the throne he had seized, was not among them. Eteocles was found, locked with Polynices in a final convulsive embrace of love and hate. They had spitted each other on each other's swords. During the night the dogs had mangled them, so there was no telling one body from the other save by their armor.

Creon donned the cloak of kingship and came out of the palace to address the people.

"Now the gods have brought our city safe through years of storm to tranquility at last. I, next of kin, am left to rule alone the kingdom to which I now lay claim. You know me. I have been among you long as fellow-citizen and loyal courtier. But no touchstone so tests the mind and heart of a man as does the practice of authority and rule."

Under the shade of his helmet's rim Creon's eyes surveyed the waiting crowd. He had them. They were settled, in the luxurious relaxation that follows an ecstacy of hate or love. Now he must seal his hold. All his life had led him to this moment. He chose his words carefully.

"I have always held that a king unwilling to seek advice is damned by inward fear, and that no less damned is he who puts private friend above his country's good. As the gods are my witness, whenever I see danger threatening my people, I shall proclaim it. No one who is Thebes's enemy shall be my friend. Our country is our life. I call you all to put loyalty to Thebes above all else."

Creon swept a gracious arm toward the elders nearest him. "These loyal counselors I call especially to conference. They were loyal subjects in the days when Laius reigned and when King Oedipus so wisely ruled us." For only a second he paused, assessing the reaction. Was that accepted? Yes. It was time that Oedipus's reputation was reinstated, if he wanted to eliminate any potential rivals by joining Haemon and Antigone in marriage. "And upon Oedipus's fall, they faithfully served his sons," he went on smoothly, "until rivalry blotted out brotherly love. Now two princes of Thebes have fallen in a single day—both slayers, both slain. One honorably defending his homeland, one in treachery. And so I, your king, now issue proclamation. . . ."

Creon's voice rose in the cadences of kingship. Antigone, listening, wondered bitterly how long and often he had practiced for this moment when the throne was his indisputably, with no challengers. She glanced at Ismene, but Ismene was merely listening attentively. Where was Haemon? Somewhere with the army; Haemon would be head of the army, with Eteocles gone. Haemon would be king next, after Creon.

"... concerning the sons of Oedipus, as follows: Prince Eteocles, who died defending his great city, shall be honored with all the rites due to the noble dead. Even now his body is being carried to this square, and all of Thebes shall join in his burial. But Polynices—"

No title given now, only contempt.

"—Polynices, who returned from exile with a vile plot to destroy his own city, and his city's gods . . . to drink the blood of his kin, and to make them slaves. . . ."

Something inside of Antigone twisted coldly. No, that was not Polynices, that never was Polynices, not even he was that hideously ashamed of their father's sins. Polynices never lifted a hand to help them, but not to harm them either. As for Eteocles . . . it was the *throne* they both wanted, the throne, focus of all longing for power, and of all their pride.

". . . for him there shall be no grave, no burial, no mourning. He who scorned our city's gods shall not have their blessing. He shall lie as he is, where he is—outside the city, unburied, carrion for dogs and vultures. A horror for all to see, and so a lesson for all who think to usurp the throne of the dragon's seed. Already a guard has been set about the corpse. If any dishonor Thebes by attempting funeral honors for this enemy, then burial—which apparently they must value highly—shall be theirs."

Creon raised his arm. The trumpets sounded. He swept into the palace that now was his, accompanied by the counselors, followed by Eurydice, the queen, and her attendants.

Haemon was with the royal party. He saw Antigone and tried to stop but was not able, because the ceremony inexorably carried him along. And because, as he approached, Antigone turned away.

XIV

The scent of incense, and the smell of battle, still lingered over Thebes in the hour before dawn. It was yet dark; not the faintest glimmer of false light paled the sky, but the dawn star shone far off, cool and serene. In the walled garden, summer flowers lifted a poignant counterpoint of hope. Antigone's bare feet made no sound nor mark on the springing herbs beneath.

Where was Ismene? Ismene must come soon or it would be too late. Must come alone, so they would not be heard nor seen—did she understand that? There had only been chance for the slightest whispered message yesterday; they had never been alone. Servants had been everywhere, and Eurydice, kindly yet elated at finding herself now undisputedly the queen. The palace walls had ears, and there had been no question of their sleeping anywhere but the palace; Creon was set on reclaiming Oedipus's reputation to his own advantage. And on defiling Polynices, for that same reason—

A flicker of white. Antigone's breath caught, then

relaxed. It was Ismene, still in her nightdress, hurrying on the gold sandals she ought not to have worn. "Antigone?"

"Hush. What kept you?"

"You said I must not be seen, and it was difficult." Ismene tried to conceal her yawn behind a delicate hand. "Can we not sit down? Antigone, your eyes are like black holes. Didn't you sleep?"

"I could not. I wonder that you did."

Ismene looked at her, then arranged herself somewhat petulantly, on the thyme-scented ground. "Did you get me out here just to speak in riddles?"

Antigone bit back a retort. Ismene was—Ismene, and dear. She dropped down beside her, grasping her sister's hands. "There is no pain, no sorrow, shame, dishonor we have not shared together, is there? Will you share with me now?"

Ismene's lovely eyes looked at her, bewildered. "What are you talking of? We have no more shame now. You heard Creon speak of our father at last with honor—"

"I heard our uncle declare for one of your brothers a state funeral with all public show, and for the other—" Antigone could not go on. The stone that was her heart was in her throat, choking her. Ismene's arms went around her, brushing back her hair gently from her burning brow.

"I know. You mustn't think of it. It's what's necessary, to keep the peace."

"It's what's necessary to doom Polynice's spirit to eternal torment. Is that our noble uncle's aim?"

They gazed at each other, and the image Antigone's

words had conjured, sum of all their childhood lessons, hung between them. The dead whose passage into Hades was not prepared by respectful hands, prescribed ceremonial rites and prayers were doomed to wander the earth forever as tormented shades. To withold such rites was an offense against the dead, against their living kin, against the gods. Ismene shrugged. "Creon's never been religious."

"Neither was Polynices, yet—Ismene, don't you remember, what he said to us at Colonus after Father cursed him? He knew then, didn't he?"

What a cursed blessing, to be afflicted by the gods with second sight. Part of the curse upon the house of Oedipus—and she was of that house; was that why, these last days, she had been webbed with shadows, with a sense of horrors she could not name?

Ismene said anxiously, "You must not think like this." Ismene, who had always been able, as she was not, to adapt to what *was,* to shake off what might be. . . . Antigone rose, her voice hard.

"It was against you and me our uncle made that order. Mostly against me. He's always hated the thought of Haemon and me eventually marrying—even when he agreed to it out of politics. And now he sees his chance to rid himself of me, to dishonor the last of our father's kin."

"Creon wasn't thinking of us. He scarcely knows us—"

"He knows we are the daughters of Oedipus and Jocasta, royal descendants of the dragon's seed! He ought to know I could not obey that blasphemous order! It would be an offense to the gods and to our blood!"

"Antigone!" Ismene's eyes were wide with terror. Antigone swung round on her, impatient anger rising.

"You said you were one with me. Are you?"

"You mean—"

"I mean to perform the sister's duty our brother asked. Will you help me?"

"Bury the body?" Ismene's hands grabbed her and pulled her down. "You're mad. Creon will kill you."

"I can't think of that."

"Oh, Antigone—" Ismene, so often childlike, sounded infinitely old. "Don't you remember what it was really like in the old days? Our father perishing in shame and misery, his eyes self-blinded? And our mother, *his* mother, dead on a rope at her own hands? And now our brothers, bearing out the curse . . . There has been enough blood. Polynices never cared about us. He never risked his life for us."

"That doesn't matter."

"If you won't think of yourself or me, think of Haemon."

"That doesn't matter either." The words came without out Antigone's volition, but as she heard them she knew them to be true. What she had said earlier was true. She was the daughter of Oedipus and Jocasta, a child of the dragon's teeth, and their curse or blessing was that red thing within them that drove them to ask hard questions, and to do what they had to do, no matter what the price.

The question she had to ask and answer was whether she could live with herself if she dishonored by inaction her family and the gods. And the thing she had to do. . . .

In a strange calm she turned. "I am not angry. And I am not judging. I only ask, once more—will you come with me?"

"I can't." Ismene was weeping. "I'm only a woman . . . I'm not strong enough to fight the state."

"Very well. I won't ask again." Is this what Father felt like, Antigone wondered oddly, on that day when he knew everything at last, his destiny? She picked up the night-dark cloak she had brought and wrapped it around her. Ismene, in a burst of terror, plucked at it.

"You must not! You'll fail—"

"At least I shall have tried."

"There is no point in endangering yourself in a hopeless cause—"

"If you tempt me with such thoughts, you'll make me hate you." Already the sky was paling. Antigone snatched up the bundle she had prepared. Holy oil, garlands, the fewest things acceptable for sacrifice.

"You're mad."

"Oh, let me alone!" Antigone burst out in sudden anger and tore herself away.

The scullery door would be barred but not guarded; the slave whose duty that was usually fell asleep. Antigone knew that, as she knew many palace secrets, knew that the narrow door in the North Gate was likewise vulnerable. Especially this night, when Thebes was safe, when everyone from high to low had celebrated the deliverance with Dionysus's rites of wine.

The stench of death was everywhere outside the walls, after two days' heavy heat. Antigone choked, nauseated, and covered her nose and mouth with her dark cloak. Most of the bodies had been gathered up—Creon had allowed not only the Thebans but the enemies as well to claim their corpses for the appropriate rites. All but Polynices'.

She found it at last, outside the Neistai Gate, so mangled that she knew it only by the Sphinx-symbol on the armor. Maggots had invaded the festering place where Eteocles' sword had found a home, and the face. . . . She turned away, retching.

Off to one side, two vultures waddled grotesquely, watching.

She wished she had water to rinse her mouth. But there was only the flask she had brought for the gods' libation, and that must be saved. When she was able, she approached the body.

The guards were a way apart, unmilitarily sleeping. She made no sound, and her feet made no trace on the hard earth. So hard, she could only scratch with her fingernails, gathering dust that she could sprinkle on the bloated corpse. It was the ritual act, not the quantity, that mattered. If she kept her face covered, did not lift her eyes, it was not so bad. She whispered the prayers, poured the libations, laid the garlands. Then she was gone, as silently and tracelessly as she had come.

The sky was growing pale as she slipped back into the palace, hiding her cloak near the door lest she should need it. Not until she was back in her own chamber did she dare let down her guard and sob into the silken pillow. She was safe. If servants found her weeping, they would assume it was in grief. When what she had done became known, Creon would surely guess, but he would not dare raise a hand against a royal princess without proof. *She was safe.*

She slept now, as one who had been drugged.

The morning sun was bright when the news reached Creon. The guard to whom the unenvied task of messenger fell by lot was in no hurry to bring such information to the king's outraged ears. He dawdled on the way, stopping to think and to rehearse.

By the time he reached the council chamber, his speech was overgarrulous and letter-perfect.

"If I am out of breath, my lord, forgive me. I knew if your lordship heard the news from another man, my head's as good as off—"

Creon demanded, impatiently, what was the matter.

"The corpse, sir . . . somebody's gone and buried it."

"What!"

"Not to say buried, really. Just some dust sprinkled. And no sign of a pick, nor scratch of shovel, either. More like somebody passing by, not knowing your lordship's order, stopped to say a prayer. Out of pity, like."

"And why did neither you nor your fellows see him?"

The sentry avoided that by pretending not to hear. "There were no tracks of an animal either, sire. We looked. And then—well, we fell to accusing one another, and 'most came to blows, till each of us was ready to take hot iron in hand and swear by the gods that we knew nothing of it. But then that stopped when somebody thought of something made our blood run cold. We had to tell you. So we drew lots and—here I am." He shifted his weight, glancing about uneasily.

A sensation, too familiar and too often disowned, gripped at Creon's vitals. He had been defied. Again, someone had challenged his authority, his right to rule. Beneath the elderly calm and majesty, the youth who had not dared the Sphinx struggled for recognition.

He must never again let indecision be born of weakness. He had known that yesterday, and so had issued his decree.

It had been defied, and soon all Thebes would know it. No use thinking of stopping, by death or bribery, the mouths of all four guards. This fellow had blurted out the news before all the council chamber.

The chief advisor said, "My lord, I fear—I feared from the first—this may be the gods' work."

Defiance of his rule, however courteous, among his own council. Creon snapped, "Don't be an old fool. I suppose the gods hold in high esteem the man who came to ransack their own temples and destroy the laws?" His mind was working furiously. "No, there's still a party of malcontents in Thebes, rebels against me. They've hired someone to do this—disgusting act." He rose. "They shall be found. And punished. Upon my oath, I swear it! You, sentry—return to your post. Sweep clean the body. And then either your detail finds who perpetrated the outrage, or I'll have you all on the rack for collaborating."

"Sire, it's not I, but he who broke your law, who has offended you—"

"Enough! You have your orders!"

The sentry left, but being a prudent man he did not return to the place where Polynices' body festered. He took the road to Corinth instead.

By midday the news had spread. *Polynices . . . Polynices' body . . . the king's death-penalty decree has been defied.* . . . There were those who felt the decree had been unwise, who felt that the ritual sprinkling was a small thing to permit to placate the gods, and Creon heard this. Antigone heard that the pitiful heap of dust had been removed, and the red mist rose in her until her blood hammered like thunder in her ears.

She was alone save for servants when she heard it. Ismene, through whatever instinct for self-preservation, had kept clear of her, and Eurydice was busy with many duties. Haemon . . . where he was, she did not know. She dared not let herself think of Haemon, or she would grow weak.

She did not think at all. She could not think. She could only run, run through the mist that choked her to whatever waited.

The guards were camped on the hill on the windward side, keeping well clear of the stench. The sun flamed high, and the heat was blazing. That was why, of course, they did not see her, a slight figure like a mirage in the blazing light.

This time, she had brought a handful of earth from the walled garden. She poured it out, not even flinching now from the sight and feel and smell of carrion. She poured out of the fine bronze urn three libation offerings, to Polynices and to the gods.

As she finished, a storm of dust, like a plague from heaven, swept down. It filled her eyes, battered her, stripped the leaves from the trembling trees. Stripped the earth and offerings again from the rotting body. She was left like a woman ravished; all at once she was screaming, shaking her fists against the sky. She was weeping and cursing, not just for Polynices, but for all of her doomed House, for father and mother and the rites she had not been able to complete for Oedipus, nor now for Polynices.

Nothing but the swirling mists was real, and she no longer cared who heard. The soldiers heard. The soldiers, not about to be caught napping again, dragged her to Creon—although, mindful of her royal position and their own danger, by a surreptitious way.

Creon at first would not believe, and when he was forced to, ordered the guards to wait alone in the next chamber and locked the door.

Across the space of the council chamber, seat of royal authority, niece and uncle faced each other. *At last,* Antigone thought. *It's been coming to this, hasn't it, ever since the day of the soothsayer, when my world collapsed, and I ran to him, and he took over. When he did not reckon, nor did I, what it meant for me to be a princess of the House of Thebes.*

When Creon spoke, his voice was oddly ordinary, as though he were questioning her over some girlish prank.

"Did you do it?"

"Yes."

Creon shot a wary glance toward the door beyond which the guards were waiting, then pulled her toward where a velvet hanging muted sound. "Now tell me, quickly. Didn't you know I'd issued an order forbidding his burial?"

"I knew it."

"Then why by all that's holy did you dare—"

"Because it was the order of a mortal man. I didn't think it strong enough to overthrow the laws of gods. And I was more afraid of disobeying them than you."

That was part of it, but not all. She could no more pin her reasons down than Creon could, though she knew he sensed them. His eyes searched hers. "You thought you wouldn't be punished because you were my niece? You didn't know the penalty, of course—by heaven, I vowed I'd have whoever attempted burial buried alive."

"I know. I knew it then."

"Are you *trying* to make me kill you?"

"No. It simply doesn't matter. Not compared to doing what I had to do."

It was as if the voice of Oedipus rang out suddenly in

the room. For a moment, both were silent. Then Creon
flung his cloak aside and ran his fingers through his hair.
"If no one knows . . . they brought you by the back way,
didn't they? I can stop their mouths. If you haven't told
anyone—"

"Are you going to kill everyone who guesses, Uncle?"

"By the gods, it will give me pleasure to kill you if you
go on like that!" Creon roared, then reined in his voice
swiftly. "Your father's daughter! When will you ever learn
that caution and moderation are virtues to be cultivated?
Especially by women—and proud thoughts do not sit well
in subordinates."

"I am my father's child. You said so, Creon! And we
of the House of Thebes do what we have to do, even if we
are weak women!"

The image of Jocasta rose between them. Jocasta the
exquisite, wed as a child to one king, surrendering her child
to save his life; wedding a young stranger at her city's
bidding. Jocasta, stoically making a noose of her own girdle.

Creon the king, Creon the powerful, was looking at
her directly, probably for the first time.

"Hasn't there been enough blood?"

"I don't know." Antigone took a deep breath. "I don't
understand it, any more than you. My brother killed his
enemy my brother. They were still brothers to each other,
and to me. All I know is we have a duty to the dead."

"Not to give equal honor to good and bad."

She shook her head, suddenly terribly tired. "There's

nothing we can say to each other, really, is there? That may be your law. It may even be the law in the Kingdom of the Dead. But it's not mine."

"By heaven," Creon said hoarsely, "we'll have no woman's law here while I live."

A shouting outside the door. The sound of something falling; a high shrill scream. And then a soldier's cursing, and Ismene, all dishevelled, came bursting in. Ismene as Antigone had never seen her, half-possessed.

"Antigone shall not suffer all the blame! It's my doing too, I was with her in it! If you kill her, you must kill us both."

One thing, then, was irrevocably determined. There was no more secret. There could be no hushing up, not if Creon hoped to rule.

"You'll not die with me!" Was it protectiveness, or her own outraged pride speaking? Antigone did not know. It did not matter. "You had a time to choose. You chose doing nothing!"

"You're mad, both of you."

"*Yes,* with the family madness!"

"Uncle, listen!" Ismene was clutching at him desperately, pleading. "She didn't know what she was doing—the strongest minds break under such misfortunes. Surely you will not—kill your niece, your own son's bride—"

"There are other fields for him to plow," Creon snapped brutally. "No son of mine will wed so unnatural a female." He strode to the door of the antechamber and threw it open on the frightened guards. "Take these two and lock them in their chambers. The proper place for women."

Like Oedipus, he was caught on the curse of his own oath. He needed time to think.

XV

Haemon heard in the city, where he was making arrangements for Eteocles' funeral. He broke off in the midst of his ordering and raced for the palace. As he did so, rumors ran after him. By the time he reached the council chamber, he knew that unless he worked diplomatic magic, Antigone's doom was sealed.

Creon was seated in state in the company of two chief advisors. He looked up, and their glances locked.

Creon's voice was all avuncular geniality. "Well, my son, no doubt you have heard my judgment. No angry words, I hope? We are yet friends?"

"I am your son." His prayers were answered, for he was able to keep his voice respectfully controlled. Haemon swallowed and went on. "By your wise decisions, my life will be always ruled."

"Well said. A father's will should have the heart's first place. It is for such sons that men pray—obedient, loyal, ready to strike down their father's foes."

"Sire, may we speak alone?"

Creon waved a comfortable hand, and the courtiers withdrew. Haemon followed to the threshold, making sure the doors were shut, and Creon watched him. "Don't be fooled, son, by lust and a woman's wiles. You will buy cold comfort if the wife you choose is worthless, and no wound strikes deeper than love turned to hate."

The words had application beyond what was intended. Haemon steeled himself to remain calm. "Father, I'm neither wise nor clever enough to prove you wrong. Nonetheless, I have to be your watchdog in the city. Your royal frown is sufficient silencer of any word that is not for your ears. But I hear the whispers . . . pity for a poor girl doomed to the cruelest death woman ever suffered because of an honorable, a reverent action. Burying a brother killed in battle, rather than letting him lie to be food for dogs. Has such a sister not earned a crown of gold? This is not what I say," he added hastily. "Merely what I hear."

"The girl is an enemy! Once having caught her in a traitorous act against the State, if I close my eyes I make myself a traitor, too. If I tolerate treachery at home, how can I rule abroad? Kings are bound by their own oaths! I hold to the law and will not betray it—least of all for a woman."

Pride.

Haemon found himself saying impetuously, "Father, do not let your first thought be your only one! Trees that bend against torrents live unbroken, while those who strain against them are snapped asunder. Sailors know it wise to tack and slacken sheets before a gale! How much more true for kings? Father, take time to think and put aside your anger!"

"Am I to be taught lessons at my time of life by one your age?"

"It's not a question of age, but of right and wrong!"

"You call it right to admire an act of disobedience?"

"I call it right to admire an act of honor! That's what the people of Thebes think her action was."

"The people of Thebes! Since when do I take orders from the people?"

Haemon looked at him. "Isn't that a childish thing for a king to say?"

"I *am* king. Responsible only to myself and to maintain the kingdom. Which is why I do this—"

"A one-man state?"

Creon loomed to his feet. "Every state belongs to its ruler, and he to it. You had better learn that before you inherit. Of course, if you're on the woman's side—"

"I'm on *your* side! *And* hers, and mine, and the gods of the dead! I only speak against you because I know that you are wrong! What sort of respect tramples on all that's holy?"

"Enough!" Creon swung out his arm, knocking one of the bronze stanchions and sending it crashing to the ground. "You'll never marry her this side of death."

"Then if she dies, she shall not die alone."

"Is that a threat?"

"Take it any way you please." Haemon stared at him, chest heaving. "Oh, Father, I could call you mad, were you not my father!"

"By all the gods of heaven, I'll make you sorry!" A

rage rose in Creon, an intolerable rage that turned the frescoed room into a cage, suffocating his lungs even as he cried out. "Guards! Bring out the she-devil and take her out to die! Now, while her bridegroom sees it done!"

Haemon did not see. He stumbled from the room, whispering hoarsely that Creon would never look on him again.

They took her out from her chamber with bridal-garlands in her hair, garlands such as Jocasta once had worn. A bride of death, on her way to subterranean marriage-bed. The sun was low in the sky, and torches burned along the palace walls. Ismene did not see. Ismene had collapsed, fainting, and been carried away by the old women, forgotten, not a part of Creon's rage. Eurydice saw; Eurydice had woven the garlands, but she did not dare reach out as the cortege passed her.

Out from the palace they brought her, out from the chamber where Jocasta had slain herself and Oedipus put out his eyes. Out past the great altar where so many fatal pronouncements had been made. Out, and down the streets to the Neistai Gate. All along the way black-robed people, daring the king's wrath, waited, and knelt as she passed by. A dirge went up for the daughter of the royal house.

Antigone's heavy eyes fell on them. She accepted a flower a weeping woman pressed into her hand, but she had no tears. She could understand, now, Oedipus in his last hour, grieving not for himself but for those who remained behind.

Haemon. Would Haemon ever understand?

They led her to a cave in the rocks, looking out across the plain, green with olives. Out toward the road down which Oedipus once had come, down which Oedipus had slain Laius. Down toward Delphi, where the prophecy that led to a blood-stained family history had first been made. Fate—or prediction of the family's own dragon-nature and dragon-pride? The gods alone knew; perhaps it didn't matter. Perhaps what mattered was not what *happened,* but how one met it. The grace with which one accepted things that could not be changed. Oedipus had learned that at last. Had she? She didn't know.

She had asked what she had to ask, done what she had to do. Oedipus would know that, and Jocasta. She would see them soon, in the Kingdom of the Shades. Jocasta—from whom she had so long been separated. And Eteocles and Polynices—together now, brothers again in death.

They were more real to her now than the living. Ismene. Creon. Haemon.

Haemon.

They led her into the cave as the sun was sinking, where Death, not Haemon, would claim her maidenhood. She stood, like a dumb animal before the altar, infinitely weary.

They began to pile the rocks before the cave's mouth. From a tree a nightingale began an early ode. A breeze lifted, bringing a wave of scent from the olive groves, heartbreakingly sweet. Far to one side she could just see the corner of the Theban wall. Thebes, her loved city.

The stones rose higher. Soon there would be no more light. But for now, beyond the opening growing ever smaller, there was the sunset, more like sunrise in all its glory. She fingered her girdle, embroidered red and gold as had been Jocasta's.

Unbelievably, a hand touched her shoulder. Antigone whirled in terror. *Haemon*. Haemon, taking her into his arms.

The last stone went into place.

Outside, the sky over Thebes was like the dawn.

XVI

With the brass-colored morning Tiresias came. Tiresias, the blind prophet, half as old as time. Straight to the palace he went, leaning on the arm of his boy guide, and on that troubled day none dared prevent him.

He found Creon in the council room, among the elders. Creon, mindful of onlookers, greeted him courteously.

"Welcome, father Tiresias. You bring me news?"

"News indeed, and advice, if you can heed it. Mark me, O King. You stand on the precipice edge."

"Grave words," Creon said, carefully courteous, aware of a current around him. He gestured for a bench to be brought for the old man, but Tiresias ignored it, standing balanced over his stick like an aged vulture.

"At my seat of divination, where I read signs in heaven, a strange sound reached my ears. Birds in vicious combat, savage cries, the whirr of wings. Full of foreboding, I made sacrifice on the altar fire. *There was no answering flame.* Only rank juice, oozing from the flesh and dripping down. The gods did not accept the offering. And why? Because the blood that stains our shrines and altars, the blood that dogs and vultures suck, is the blood of Oedipus, spilled from his children's veins. Our fires, our prayers the gods abominate. And it is your doing."

The current in the council room was stronger. Haemon had been right. The people of Thebes did not support him. Creon forced himself to remain at ease as the old fool went on.

"Mark this, my son. All men fall into sin, no matter how wise or high in station. But he who sins is not forever lost if he makes amends, if he is not too stubborn for repentance. Only a fool is governed by self-will."

Creon's lips smiled, but his eyes did not. "So you, too, take me for a target, like the rest. I know the art of prophets, how they make kings their commodities, to trade and traffic for their own advancement. Hear you this: All the gold of India, all the silver of Sardis could not buy a tomb for yonder traitor. No, not though eagles carried his carcass to the throne of Zeus!"

It had not been wise to say that. To some of the conservatives around him, it was blasphemy. Tiresias swayed forward. In the torchlight his shadow grew ominously against the wall, and his blind eyes glittered. "Then hear this. Before the chariot of the sun has rounded his wheeling way, you shall give blood of your blood up to death. Two debts to pay—one for the dead lying dishonored above the ground, one for the life unjustly sent to death. You cannot alter this. The gods themselves cannot. It follows of necessity from your own actions." Tiresias' voice was like a knife. "Do I speak this for my own gain? The time is coming when this house of death shall echo with the wails of doom. Take me home, boy. We'll leave the son of the dragon to vent his dragon-wrath on younger ears."

They went, and not a hand was raised to stop them.

Creon's wrath did not break. Creon was silent. It was the chief among the counselors who spoke, in a tone firmer than he would previously have taken.

"I have never known that man's prophecies to prove false."

Creon knew. Creon was reliving what he had buried for years—the coming of Tiresias to Oedipus. Oedipus's pride. Oedipus's outrage. Oedipus's error in accusing him. Oedipus's error in perceiving himself innocent.

Creon's voice said what it had not said in years. "What must I do?"

The men in the council chamber exchanged glances. It was the leader who replied. "Release the woman from the cave. Set up a tomb for the one who lies unburied."

He must do it. There was no armor against necessity.

Whether it was the necessity of the gods, or his subjects, was a matter he would not wrestle with till later.

Creon clapped his hands.

"Slaves! Guards! Bring spades and shovels! My mind is made."

They went out of the palace, out through the Onka Gate, and all Thebes saw them. They came first to the place where lay the thing that had once been a body, and they offered prayers to the goddess of roads, and to Pluto god of the Underworld. They washed the dog-mauled corpse with holy water, and on a fire of fresh-cut branches burned what was left, raising over the ashes a mound of Theban earth.

Then they went on to the cavern in the rocks. A strange foreboding lay upon the landscape and touched them all. Faster and faster they pulled off the rocks, and at the end Creon was clawing at them with his own hands. At last a passage in the stones was clear. Those nearest looked, but could not speak of what they saw.

It was Creon who went within, Creon who saw Antigone, like Jocasta, hanging from a noose of red and gold. And on his knees, his arms embracing his lost bride, Haemon, dead on the point of his own sword. It was Creon who cut Antigone down; Creon who carried his son, blood of his blood, back to the palace of death.

The news traveled before them, as such things will. A self-appointed messenger ran through the streets. *Hear, all of Cadmus' city, hear and weep! Disaster on the royal house. Death, and the guilt on living heads. . . . All has happened, as the prophet said.*

Eurydice was just on her way to prayer at the temple of Athene. She stopped, one delicate hand on the temple's door latch, and listened. Without a word she went back to the palace, stepping quickly on her high-arched feet.

She went to her private altar, still not speaking, and with a gesture commanded her maids to leave. Then she picked up the sacrificial knife with both her hands and drove its sharp point home into her heart. As darkness dimmed her eyes, she broke her silence, calling upon her dead to welcome her, and with her last breath cursing Creon as their slayer.

Creon, carrying Haemon in his arms, was greeted by the news at the high altar.

You cannot alter fate. The gods themselves cannot. It follows of necessity from your own actions. He could alter nothing, could say nothing. In silence, Creon laid Haemon down before the altar and went into the palace; and all the shades of his blood-stained, pride-stained family went with him. With no companionship save theirs, he climbed up to the parapet from which, long ago, he had seen Oedipus the young hero wrestling with the Sphinx to gain the city's throne. Beyond lay Polynices' pyre, the tomb-cave, the crossroads where Laius had fallen, Delphi. The places that marked the days of a dynasty, born of pride and blood, of reason and unreason.

Tiresias had known, as the Sphinx had known. Humankind was born in ignorance, and in the flower of its strength it stood upright and dared the heavens, but only with age and suffering came the wisdom that knew one must not rely on one's own strength alone.

He wished he could blind himself to knowledge, as Oedipus had done. He wished for the release of death. But he was Creon, and not a man of action—this day's sorrows had proved how ill-advised action could be. He had wished to be king, and now he was king. That was his fate. The future was not known, but in the hands of the gods. Whatever was to be, he could not escape.

Creon went back into the palace, his head bowed. Behind him the sky over Thebes was the color of doom.

AUTHOR'S NOTES

When you read the story of the Royal House of Thebes, you are reading fiction, not history. In the same way, Athenian audiences in the fifth century B.C. attending Sophocles' plays about the Thebans, upon which this book is largely based, went to the theater—to a playwriting contest, actually—not to a history lesson. They already knew the lives of Oedipus and Jocasta, Antigone and Creon as well as we know the stories of Cinderella, the Sleeping Beauty and such American legends as Paul Bunyan and Johnny Appleseed.

To the Greeks, the tales of royal families of the past were myths, and they were valued as myth, not history. That is, they were told and retold because the truths of human nature they contained were more important than whether the story was or was not literally true. There certainly was a Royal City of Thebes; there may or may not have been a king named Oedipus. That his story has endured more than three thousand years (it was old when Sophocles dramatized it) tells us there's something in it more significant than when (or whether) a certain ruler was born, and ruled, and died.

The Greeks judged their playwrights much as we judge songwriters today: How much originality have they brought to familiar themes and established musical forms? What new insight can they reveal about the state of being human? There are contradictions within Sophocles' plays, which were written over a long span of years, and between them and other versions of the Oedipus story. Who is older, Oedipus or Creon? Polynices or Eteocles? The tales conflict; I have chosen to write according to what seemed most logical to me. Was Creon king, or regent, between the death of Laius and the coming of Oedipus; between Oedipus' departure and his sons' claiming the throne? Did Jocasta actually have equal authority with Oedipus in Thebes, as the plays imply? Greek audiences did not care about such points.

What they cared about was whether or not the myths stretched their minds and purged their hearts by the experiencing of pity and of fear. They cared about whether or not they came into a better understanding of themselves, each other, nature, and the divine. They cared about learning how disharmonious humans could live in harmony with their universe. They wanted to know how to live their public and private lives, how to make choices in a world that was not absolute black and absolute white but multishaded.

The story of Oedipus raises profound questions. (One of the most enduring being, "If gods and oracle doomed Oedipus to the crimes that he committed, if he could not escape them, then why should he be held accountable and guilty?") The characters themselves raise them . . . as Antigone says, in Jean Anouilh's play of that name, "I come from a race of people who ask hard questions, and who must keep on asking them to the bitter end." In the plays, the silence that answers the questions is like thunder.

In this book, I have not attempted answers, either. Because the plays do not. Because I am human and to try to "speak what the gods alone know" would be presumptuous. But more, because I believe with the Greeks—and with the mythmakers of many cultures—that the answer is not important. What matters, in myth after myth, religion after religion, is *asking the right question*.

I have heard the Old Testament Book of Job described, with irreverent reverence, as "Man asking God, 'Why?' and God responding, 'You're asking the wrong question.'" Not *why* does man suffer, *why* does man fail, *why* is he so often captive of his own worst impulses, *why* is he so often forced to choose the lesser of two evils? But *how* does he make the choice, *how* does he live with himself and others and his gods in a universe he but dimly understands, *how* does he find the peace in the eye of the hurricane?

I submit that the universality of those *why* questions, and the *how* that is their answer, are the secret of the durability of the Oedipus myth. And that they are more important than the intriguing question of whether Oedipus actually lusted for his mother. It mattered little to Oedipus on the Day of the Soothsayer whether he needed to feel guilty or not. He simply *did*, and it was not till he made peace with the warring tides within him that he could be free. Oedipus, blind, was given the gift of insight.

Archibald MacLeish, in the closing speech of *J.B.*, his dramatic retelling of the Book of Job, deals with the unanswerable questions in this way:

> We can never know. He answers me with the
> stillness of a star that silences my asking.
> We are, and that is all our answer. We are,
> and what we are can suffer. But what suffers,
> *loves.* . . .

Perhaps that is the ultimate answer to the human condition, and it rings through the inner silence of all potent myths.

As psychologist Rollo May says of creative people, who have the gift of what the Greeks called the "divine madness," "They do not run away from non-being, but by encountering and wrestling with it, force it to produce being. They knock on silence for an answering music; they pursue meaninglessness until they force it to mean."

That is what Oedipus and Antigone do for me.

GLOSSARY

AEGEAN SEA the part of the Mediterranean Sea that lies between Greece on the north and west and Turkey on the east.

AEGEUS King of Athens and father of Theseus. According to legend, the Aegean Sea was named for him because he threw himself into it believing his son had been killed by the Minotaur.

ANTIGONE daughter of Oedipus and Jocasta, sister of Eteocles, Polynices and Ismene.

APHRODITE goddess of love and beauty. (Roman: Venus)

APOLLO god of prophecy, the arts, healing, light and truth, music, archery. Son of Zeus and Leto, born on the Isle of Delos. Purifier, peacemaker, masculine ideal of beauty, intelligence, strength. Spoke through the oracle of Delphi. Because the god of light, often identified as god of the sun. Drove chariot of the sun across the sky. Also called Phoebus.

ARES god of war, son of Zeus and Hera. (Roman: Mars)

ARGOS town in southern Greece, in district once called Argolis. About 9 miles NW of Nauplia and the coast.

ARTEMIS goddess of the chase, protector of wild animals, the "divine huntress," also identified with the moon as her brother Apollo was identified with the sun. Daughter of Zeus and Leto. (Roman: Diana)

ATHENA goddess of wisdom, daughter of Zeus (sprang full-grown from his brain at the Tritonian Lagoon in Libya). Patroness of arts and crafts. (Roman: Minerva)

ATHENS capital of Greece, about 5 miles inland from seaport of Piraeus in east central Greece, at the SW end of the Attic Peninsula. Sacred to Athena, who was its patroness. It was known in the ancient world as a center of enlightenment.

AURORA the goddess of the dawn.

BOEOTIA province north of Athens in which the city of Thebes is located.

BOURRAIAI GATE the northern gate to the city of Thebes.

CADMUS founder and King of Thebes in Boeotia. Sister of Europa who was kidnapped by Zeus; while searching for her he abandoned that pursuit and founded Thebes on the instructions of the Delphic oracle. Married Harmonia, daughter of Ares and Aphrodite; father of Ino, Semele, Agave, Autonoe. His descendants intermarried with the descendants of the Sparti, who sprang from the teeth of the dragon Cadmus killed. Both Cadmus and the Sparti, therefore, were ancestors of the Royal House of Thebes.

CHALKIS city northeast of Thebes, one of the busiest and most important of ancient Greece. Famous for its metalwork, especially in bronze, and for the purple dye derived from seashells.

CHITON a long tubular garment of wool or linen, occasionally silk, worn by men and women. Frequently fastened at the shoulders by brooches.

CITHAERON a wild, rugged mountain in Boeotia, sacred to Zeus and Dionysus, home of the Furies and of wild beasts. Unwanted children were frequently exposed on it to die and were often rescued by shepherds who grazed flocks on the mountainsides.

COLONUS village 1½ miles NW of Athens, sacred to the Furies in their benevolent aspect as the Eumenides or Kindly Ones. The birthplace of Sophocles, who described it in *Oedipus at Colonus*.

CORINTH major city "in the corner of Argos" in the Peloponnesus, near the Isthmus and Gulf of Corinth.

CREON son of Menoeceus of Thebes, a descendant of the Sparti; brother of Jocasta, Queen of Thebes. Father of Haemon and husband of Eurydice.

DAULIA (also Daulis) city in Phocis, about 12 miles E of Delphi.

DELPHI shrine near Mt. Parnassus, called "earth's navel-stone," thought by Greeks to be the center of the earth. Most sacred and most famous shrine to Apollo and site of his oracle.

DELPHIC ORACLE priestess who presided over shrine at Delphi. Apollo's messages were thought to be transmitted to her while she was in a trance caused by vapor rising through cleft in rocks, possibly augmented by smoke from burning drugs; her unintelligible syllables were translated by a listening priest.

DIONYSUS god of wine and the fruits of the vine, and of ecstasy. Son of Zeus and Semele, the daughter of Cadmus. Associated with the two results of wine: freedom and ecstatic joy; savage brutality. A fertility god identified with a death-and-resurrection cult and with the emotional frenzy of the Maenads. Also god of the theater; the first tragedies were performed in his honor. (Roman: Bacchus)

DORIANS one of the traditional branches of the ancient Greek people, who came from the north and during the Dark Age of Greece (1200 B.C.–750 B.C.) conquered most of the other Greek kingdoms. Under the Dorians the concept of city-states (city + surrounding countryside = kingdom) developed.

ELEKTRA GATE southeast gate to Thebes, near where Cadmus sowed the dragon's teeth.

ETEOCLES son of Oedipus and Jocasta; brother of Polynices, Ismene and Antigone.

EUMENIDES another name for the Furies in their aspect as benevolent conscience; means "kindly ones."

EUROPA the sister of Cadmus, who was abducted by Zeus and transformed into a white heifer to hide her from Hera's jealousy.

EURYDICE the wife of Creon and mother of Haemon.

FURIES the Eumenides, born of the blood of Uranus when he was slain by his son, the Titan Cronus. They lived in the Underworld, where they punished evildoers, and also pursued sinners upon earth—especially those who transgressed against the unwritten laws of instinct and blood loyalty (killing a blood relative, violating sanctuary, killing a guest, etc.). Traditionally considered inexorable but just—possibly personifications of conscience. Usually portrayed as three women: Tisiphone, Megaera, Alecto.

GREAT MOTHER in ancient cultures, the goddess of birth and fertility, an almost universal concept. The Greeks identified her with the Titan Rhea, and later her cult became fused with those of Artemis and Aphrodite.

HADES 1) one name for the king of the Underworld and husband of Persephone; 2) the Underworld itself, the kingdom of the dead, which lay beneath the secret places of the Earth. Divided into three regions: Tartaros, the place of torment; Erebus or Acheron, the vale of shadows; Elysium, the place of blessedness.

HAEMON prince of Thebes, son of Creon and Eurydice; cousin and fiancé of Antigone.

HARMONIA daughter of Ares and Aphrodite and wife of Cadmus.

HECTARE unit of square measure; 2.471 acres.

HELLAS Greece

HELLENES the Greek people.

HERA sister-wife of Zeus, queen of the gods. Protector of marriage and married women; known for her jealousy and long-held grudges. (Roman: Juno)

HOMOLOIS GATE gate on the east side of Thebes.

ISMENE daughter of Oedipus and Jocasta, sister of Eteocles, Polynices and Antigone.

JOCASTA Queen of Thebes, daughter of Menoceus and sister of Creon; wife first of Laius and then of Oedipus; mother of Eteocles, Polynices, Ismene and Antigone.

KINDLY ONES see *Eumenides*.

KRENEAI GATE gate on SW side of Thebes, near Spring of Ares.

LABDACUS son of Polydorus, the son of Cadmus; King of Thebes and father of Laius.

LAIUS King of Thebes, son of Labdacus (see above); husband of Jocasta. Killed at "the place where three roads meet."

LETHE the "river of forgetfulness" in the Underworld; whoever drank of it lost memory as a result.

MEGARON the great central hall of a Greek palace where guests were entertained.

MENOCEUS father of Creon and Jocasta, and a descendant of the Sparti.

MEROPE Queen of Corinth, wife of Polybus and mother to Oedipus.

NEMESIS the goddess of retribution.

NEISTAI GATE northwest gate of Thebes, near where Eteocles and Polynices died and where Polynices' body lay.

NORTH GATE another name for Bourraiai Gate.

OEDIPUS prince of Corinth and son to King Polybus and Queen Merope. After slaying the Sphinx, became King of Thebes and married the widowed Queen Jocasta. Their children were Eteocles, Polynices, Ismene and Antigone.

OLYMPUS mountain on borders of Macedonia and Thessaly, regarded as the home of the gods.

ONKA GATE gate leading from Thebes to the road to Athens, near the sanctuary of Athena Onka where Cadmus sacrificed after killing the dragon.

ORACLE place at which ancient Greeks consulted the gods for advice or prophecy; also the person who conveys the gods' messages.

OTHERWORLD another name for Underworld.

PARNASSUS mountain about 83 miles NW of Athens, sacred to Apollo, Dionysus and the Muses; regarded as the seat of poetry and music. The shrine of Delphi is located on the slopes of Mt. Parnassus.

PERSEPHONE daughter of Demeter and wife of Pluto; Queen of the Underworld.

PHOCIS province to NW of Athens where Delphi is situated.

PHOEBUS another name for Apollo; means "the brilliant shining one."

PLUTO King of the Underworld and husband of Persephone.

POLYBUS King of Corinth, married to Merope; father to Oedipus.

POLYNICES Prince of Thebes, son of Oedipus and Jocasta and brother of Eteocles, Ismene and Antigone.

POSEIDON Olympic god, son of Cronus and Rhea; brother of Zeus; chief god of the sea and god of horses. (Roman: Neptune)

PROITOS GATE northeast gate of Thebes, near the road to Chalkis.

PROMETHEUS son of the Titan Iapetus; stole fire from the gods to give to man and was punished by Zeus by being chained to a mountain peak in the Caucasus where every day an eagle tore out his liver, which grew back by night. His name means "foresight"; he represents man's free-spirited defiance of the gods despite all costs.

PYTHIAN a term referring to the priestess who received the oracles of Apollo at Delphi; sometimes refers to Apollo himself.

SEVEN GATES OF THEBES the seven entrances to the walled city of Thebes; made famous when the "seven against Thebes"—Polynices and his allies—attacked the city, sending one general and his army against each of the seven gates. Clockwise from N, the gates were: Bourraiai, Proitos, Homolois, Elektra, Onka, Kreneai, Neistai.

SOUINON Cape Souinon, extending into the Mediterranean Sea South of Athens.

SPARTI "sown ones," the name given to the men who sprang up from the dragon's teeth, and their descendants; the Thebans.

SPHINX a creature, usually female, with human head and animal body. The Theban sphinx, which battled Oedipus, had the body of a lion, the tail of a serpent or dragon, the wings of an eagle, and the head of a woman. Famous for posing unanswerable riddles.

SPRING OF ARES spring of SW of Thebes, near Kreneai Gate, supposed to spring from cave, which was home to the dragon, sacred to Ares, that Cadmus killed.

STYX main river of five in the Underworld, so sacred that the gods took oaths by it. Only the ghosts of those properly buried could cross the Styx and gain admittance to the Underworld.

TANTALUS a king, possibly descendant of the gods, ancestor of the House of Atreus, who offended the gods by serving them a cannibal feast. He was punished in the Underworld by being forced to stand in water that receded whenever he bent to quench his thirst from it, while over his head grew grapes that always receded when he sought to feed his hunger. Thus he was forever "tantalized."

THEBES city in Boeotia founded by Cadmus, at the command of Apollo and Athena, and peopled by the Sparti, who sprang up from the teeth of Ares' dragon that Cadmus killed. Two other Thebes also existed in the ancient world: a smaller city near Pagasae and Iolcus in Thessaly, and the capital of Egypt.

THESEUS Athenian hero and king, son of Aegeus; slew the Minotaur and thus saved Athens from having to send human tribute to Crete. He was regarded as the Greek ideal of a heroic, civilized man, and embodiment of all that Athens stood for and of all the virtues of Apollo.

THESSALY a large territory in northern Greece, south of Macedonia and north of Aetolia and Locris.

TIRESIAS a blind Theban seer. According to legend, Athena struck the child Tiresias blind because he once saw her bathing, but as compensation gave him the gifts of prophecy, divination, a long life (three times the normal span), and the power to retain his mental accomplishments in the Underworld. All that he predicted always came true.

UNDERWORLD the world of the dead, ruled by Hades or Pluto; also called Hades itself. See Hades (2).

ZEUS Olympian god, son of the Titans Cronus and Rhea; husband of Hera. The supreme ruler, Lord of the Sky, the Rain-God, the Cloud-Gatherer; fount of kingly power, patron of rulers, establisher of laws, order, justice. (Roman: Jupiter)

CREDITS

Primary sources for *The Days of the Dragon's Seed* were Sophocles' plays *Oedipus Rex* (429 or 427 B.C.), *Oedipus at Colonus* (401 B.C.) and *Antigone* (422 or 421 B.C.). I have also consulted Aeschylus' *Seven Against Thebes* fragment (467 B.C.) and other early references to the Royal House of Thebes. Additional information from Larousse *Mythology* and *The New Century Handbook*.

II.

I am much indebted to Professor Timothy Renner, Chairman of Classics Department, at my own alma mater, Montclair College, Upper Montclair, New Jersey. To him I owe the liberty to ". . . use reason and imagination . . . in constructing a historical novel." According to Professor Renner, "There just are no documentary sources (except for the Linear B tablets, which . . . do not provide any matches with names or events in the literary tradition on Greek kingship in the heroic period). The Greeks of the fifth century and afterward, on whom we depend for nearly all our accounts of the Oedipus cycle, were so unused to kingship that even if they had cared to they probably could not have been very successful in painting a picture of the legal or constitutional basis of a monarch's power. . . . They venerated the kingly individuals of the Bronze Age as ancestors and sometimes demigods, but at least in the period when the great tragedians were writing very few Greeks would have accepted rule by a king or even seriously considered the idea. These factors, coupled perhaps with the fact that the tragedies are poetry, give rise to the vagueness which shrouds the questions (of historical fact)."